If you want to sign up for my newsletter and get a FREE Novella – just hit the link below. Join the tribe and have great fun with giveaways, free short stories, audio books and loads of news...

https://BookHip.com/QSLPAHD

PROJECT BLOODBORN
Book 10
WOLF MESSENGER

Chapter 1

Shadow ghosted over the snow, leaving barely a sign of her passage as she ran.

From a distance, apart from her unusual pitch-black coloring, she looked just like any other mountain lion. However, if one got closer it was immediately apparent, she was over twice the size of a normal cougar.

Over ten feet long and weighing in at almost four hundred pounds. A poem of strength and beauty. The absolute acme of supernatural evolution.

Werelion.

She halted at the top of a hill, breath steaming in the frigid air as she surveyed the valley below her.

She didn't often go out by herself, preferring to run with Brenner, or even some of the werebears that lived close by. After all, Shadow was not ostensibly a loner, she enjoyed running with her pride.

But this morning she needed some alone time.

Because this morning she had learned she was pregnant.

With Brenner's cub.

She had suspected for a few days, but it was confirmed when Grandma had visited early, while Ded was chopping wood, and the angel had told her.

Shadow didn't question the news. After all, why would Grandma lie?

After thanking the ancient Malak, Shadow had asked her not to tell Brenner yet. She would do so later. After her run.

After her moment alone.

Not that she was nervous in any way whatsoever. Shadow knew Brenner would be ecstatic. Beyond joyful.

No, she merely needed a little time to absorb the news herself before telling everyone.

As she gazed out across the valley, she stretched – and changed, assuming her hybrid form. An upright cross between human and lion. It was easier to think in this form. Less visceral. Less animal.

More human.

As she contemplated her future, she suddenly sensed a 'wrongness'. A disturbance in the aura of the forest.

Then she smelled it.

The slightest whiff of brimstone.

Her senses cycled into overdrive as adrenalin flooded her system, supercharging her muscles, her reaction times, her awareness.

Some twenty feet in front of her, a shimmering light appeared. Lengthened. Crackled. Expanded.

And opened to reveal a stygian hole, torn into the very fabric of reality.

A gateway from the darkness.

Accompanied by the sound of rolling thunder, the gateway disgorged a pack of ravening, slobbering, screeching beasts. A nightmare collection of taloned claws and multiple limbs and ragged teeth.

Black and foul and stinking they came. Scores of them, quickly surrounding her.

Shadow had seen their like before.

Demons.

The darkest denizens of hades.

She had no idea why they were there, or even how they had found her. But she knew one thing for certain – they meant to do her harm.

And in doing so, harm her unborn cub.

With a shriek of anger, she launched herself at them, claws extended, canines bared.

The demons were strong, driven by evil intent and dark and desperate powers. However, they were not fighting for the life of their child.

The dark beings attacked with no coordinated plan, they simply looked to overwhelm Shadow with weight and numbers.

She retaliated by moving fluidly from point to point. Never stopping, always attacking. Using their own numbers against them as she wove in and out of combat, slashing throats, tearing off limbs and crushing skulls.

At the same time, she howled out a mental call to her Alpha.

Though she knew he was too distant to make it in time.

Even with Brenner's prodigious speed, the fight would be over before he arrived.

Destroyed bodies lay all about her, their fetid ichor leaking from shattered limbs and torn bodies, filling the air with the stench of brimstone and rotting flesh. Shadow had dispatched over thirty demon spawn, and as a result they were keeping their distance, circling her as they looked to exploit an unguarded moment, or lapse of concentration.

Behind them, the gateway sputtered and sizzled, expanding and contacting like some obscene living doorway to darkness.

Then without warning the opening expanded and a massive demon lord strode through. Unlike the minions that had passed through before, this beast was humanoid. Albeit over ten feet tall. Deep red skin, overlong arms and legs, massive musculature and two jagged horns sweeping backwards from his forehead.

Shadow tensed herself, ready to leap back into battle.

But the demon lord held up his hand.

'Stay yourself, child,' he thundered, his voice like the crashing of an avalanche. 'You are but one, and we are legion. If you continue this pointless resistance, you shall surely perish. And in doing so, so shall your child also cease to be.'

Shadow visibly flinched at the mention of her cub. 'How did you know?'

The demon lord laughed, a sound imbued with such bitterness and cruelty it seemed to scour Shadow's mind.

'Our Father knows all. He is all, and all shall worship him.'

'Fuck you,' swore Shadow. 'I'd rather die.'

The demon shrugged. 'So be it,' he rumbled. 'Strange, I would have thought your child's life worth more to you than simple pride.'

He was about to gesture, calling the demons back into the fray when Shadow nodded. 'Okay,' she said. 'What do you want?'

'Come with us. My Master would have you visit His house.'

'And then?'

The evil messenger shrugged. 'Does it matter? You and your future progeny get to live a while longer.'

Shadow thought for a few seconds, then she nodded. The foul creature was correct. Every second she survived was one more second Brenner had to find her.

Rescue her.

And kill every single one of these cruel SOB's.

'Lead the way,' she acquiesced.

The demon lord smiled and turned to the gateway.

Shadow walked with him, through the dark opening to his master's dwelling.

As did the minions.

And then they were gone, leaving their dead, and their stench, and their filth behind them to sully the pure white snow.

Chapter 2

'You can't be a farmer,' stated Griff. 'You're a predator.'

'So?' questioned Brenner.

'So, don't be stupid.'

'Okay, then by your logic,' returned Brenner. 'If I was a ...dunno, a were-deer or were-cow I could farm, but as a wolf I can't.'

Griff chuckled. 'Nah. Even as a cow or some other vegan-type werebeast, you'd still be a predator. It's in your DNA. Killer, not nurturer.'

'Makes no sense,' sulked Brenner.

'I don't know why you two argue about such trivia,' said Grandma with a sigh. 'You don't even want to farm, Ded.'

'So?'

'Stop being an idiot.' Grandma shook her head, took out her pipe and her tabaco pouch and started fixing a smoke. She had changed her look slightly over the last few months, dialing down the nineteen-forties movie star and ramping up a more super-model vibe. There was no longer any hint of the ancient old lady look she used to present to the world.

Griff had also lost a couple more years, looking like a retired athlete in his mid-thirties as opposed to a man closer to his eighties.

Brenner looked the same. Just like he had since Vietnam.

Griff offered the big man a cigarette, but as Brenner reached out, he froze.

Then without warning he exploded into his wolfman form and charged from the room, shattering the front door as he ran straight through it. As he accelerated away, two massive wings of shade blossomed from his shoulders, like a mantle of night.

And an unholy howl of anger rent the air.

'Holy shit,' yelled Griff. 'What the hell'

'It's Shadow,' said Grandma, her voice barley a whisper. 'She's been taken. Come with me.'

She grabbed Griff by his arm, and with a gesture tore open a fracture in time and space, creating a personal portal. Then she pulled the two of them through, teleporting to the center of Backlash, just outside Colson's bar.

It was time to get the townsfolk involved in the search.

Chapter 3

Shadow groaned as she regained consciousness. Someone, or something, had struck her as she came through the gateway.

Hard.

She could feel the sticky, congealed blood covering the right side of her face.

But she could do little about it, as her hands were chained to the wall above her head. Likewise, her ankles were chained to the floor.

Thankfully she was in a seated position and not actually hanging from the chains.

She noted she was in her human form. Also, she was naked.

With a grunt of effort, she tried to change into her lion mode, aiming to shatter the steel bands as she did.

Nothing.

It was like her were-soul no longer existed.

She tried again, growling in anger and frustration.

'It will do you no good, child,' boomed a voice from the impenetrable darkness of the dungeon, on the other side of the bars. 'You are in an area of His realm now. Your paltry powers are as naught.'

'Who are you?'

'I am your new master. Your beginning and your end.'

'Fuck you,' snarled Shadow as she yanked even harder on her restraints. 'Brenner will come for me, and when he does…'

'Before he does, you shall already be dead. As will your newborn child,' countered the voice. 'There is no way he can follow us here. We are too strongly warded.'

'Why?' asked Shadow. 'What am I to you, if not bait for Brenner?'

The voice chuckled. 'Ded Brenner. That Authority is of no moment to us. The only reason he even exists is as a mere cog in the Great Plan. And now we have circumvented that part of the plan by taking you.'

'I don't get it,' admitted Shadow.

'Of course you don't, you ignorant girl. And I have no reason to enlighten you. However, as I know the knowledge will bring you pain, I shall explain. You and your mate are nothing more than a pair of breeders. Your false god's ineffable plan was to get you together for one reason only. So you could bear the child currently in your womb.

'The Great Plan refers to it as – the Wolf Messenger.

'According to The Plan, your progeny will bring peace and understanding to the world. It shall unite shifters and humans against so-called evil. Blah, blah and so much crap. Brenner and you were to be the prodigy's parents and protectors.'

'Are you saying my child is the second coming?' gasped Shadow.

The voice howled with laughter. 'Oh, how presumptuous of you. The second coming indeed. No, the false god has only one son, and trust me, it isn't your unborn brat. No, the child of The Plan will be more like a facilitator. A politician if you would. Whatever, it would be bad news for my ilk.

'However, in his wisdom, and I use that word with no respect and a healthy dose of sarcasm, your false god decided to allow the Great Plan some degree of Freedom. Choice. He's very big on that, you know. Not like my master.

'You see, in as much as the child could grow to become a beacon for peace, the same child's blood sacrifice will ensure the unstoppable coming of the Darkness.'

'You're telling me you are going to sacrifice my child?' whispered Shadow.

'Yep,' agreed the voice. 'That's why we have to keep you alive until term. Then it's goodbye mommy. Goodbye baby. And hello Darkness my old friend.'

Shadow screamed and threw herself against the chains once more, putting everything she had into it.

But to no avail.

The voice chuckled once again and left the room on silent feet.

Chapter 4

Grandma spoke to Colson and he immediately got onto his cell and rallied the townsfolk, telling them to gather at his bar-come-diner ASAP.

In under twenty minutes the place was packed, and the hubbub of conversation filled the room.

Grandma walked up to the bar and called for silence.

'Listen up, people,' she called out, her voice clear and commanding. 'Shadow has gone missing.'

The crowd burst into discussion as they gave voice to their concern and immediately started to speculate.

'Quiet,' continued the Malak. 'Brenner is already out looking for her. We know she has been taken, but she may still be close. I'm not going to get into the how's and why's of the situation, I just need you all to help.'

There was a mumble of acceptance. The townsfolk knew more than enough about Brenner to accept that weird shit happened around him. But he was their sheriff, their protector and their friend. So, whatever was going down, they were going to help to the very best of their abilities.

Grandma started naming people and giving instructions.

'Clem, you and Brad take your snowmobiles and head west. Make sure you're both armed. In fact, that goes for all of you. Tool up. Better safe than sorry. Now, Peter, you and Joseph, same thing, go north.'

She continued instructing until everyone there knew exactly what their role was for the next twenty-four hours.

Basically, it boiled down to – find Shadow.

***

Grandma's portal crackled into being in the forest outside the were-Grizzly caves.

'Come on, old man,' she berated Griff. 'Move it, we need to speak to Barton.'

'Hey,' exclaimed Griff. 'I'm not slowing you down. Relax.'

'Can't, something real bad has happened to that little girl. We need to tell the bears. Get them working on it.'

Less than a minute later, Grandma was talking to Barton, the Grizzly Alpha. Half an hour after that, every available were-bear was scouring the surrounds for any sign of Shadow.

Chapter 5

Brenner had assumed his full wolf form mere seconds after leaving the cabin. Firstly, because when it came to running and tracking, nothing beat the wolf. And secondly, the beast allowed him to put aside human emotions and concentrate on the task at hand, as opposed to filling his mind with an overwhelming red rage.

His paws flew over the snow as he followed Shadows scent. At the same time, fear rose inside him. He couldn't feel her. And he could always feel her. A low-level pull towards wherever she was. Like his own personal loadstone.

Now, apart from her scent – nothing.

Brennerwolf howled in anguish as he ran, his voice reverberating through the forest, shivering the snow from the tees and shaking the very earth itself, such was its power.

And every wolf within a thousand miles felt his pain and howled alongside him.

Their leader was suffering, and so did they.

And just like that, wolf spoke to wolf across the state, and soon every one of them was searching for the image of Shadow that Brennerwolf had in his mind.

It didn't take Brenner long to find the scene of the battle. Frantically he swept the area, nose to the ground as he followed the ebb and flow of the battle. Then he smelled the electric energy of the gateway. Putrid, vile and distorted. A cross between rancid swamp water and freshly poured pig iron.

He had come across that same stench before.

It reeked of hell.

And he knew Shadow was gone.

Falling back onto his haunches he threw his head back and howled his pain, his fear, his anger.

And with it all, his promise of ultimate retribution.

Brennerwolf, Alpha of Alpha's, King of the shifters, fallen Angel and Authority of the Lord, was going to war.

And this time it was personal.

Chapter 6

New Orleans.

The Big Easy.

The Birthplace of Jazz.

Two old men sat at a small table in a dark corner of a bar, at the end of Bourbon Street.

Both were dark skinned with long gray hair and blue eyes. Bushy gray beards, semi formal clothing. Open necked white shirts, dark suits, patent leather shoes. The clothes were neat and clean and so threadbare you could almost pick out the individual strands of the weave.

On the table sat a clear glass bottle. Half empty.

Or maybe half full, depending on who was looking at it.

The barman didn't complain that the old men were drinking their own liquor.

In fact, he didn't even know they were there.

The Watchers were never seen, unless they willed it so.

'She has been taken,' said the one.

'This was not according to the Great Plan,' added the second.

'The Great Plan sucks.'

'Please, Mister Reeve,' scowled the second man. 'It is His Plan.'

'I always said it was far too complicated,' replied mister Reeve as he took a sip of shine.

'Yes, I admit, at times the Great Plan seems a touch ineffable, but the Messenger had to be brought to pass. And this was the best way.'

'Not any more, even we cannot see where she is. Well, not without breaking all of the rules. And how in His name did the dark one find out about the Great Plan?'

'Therein lies the biggest question,' admitted mister Bolin. 'Does heaven have a mole?'

'A mole?' scoffed mister Reeve. 'This is not the cold war, this is …' he paused as he thought. 'Actually, this is the cold war. And yes, we have uncovered traitors before. However, I suspect it has to do with free will. For has he not oft said, humanity must be free to make their own choice whether to obey or willfully choose disobedience.'

'We need to talk to Brenner.'

'The Great Plan forbids it.'

'So?'

'Just saying.'
'Okay, let's go.'

***

Brenner hulked over the table, still part man, part wolf. His breathing heavy, yellow eyes filled with rage.

Griff sat opposite him, and Grandma stood with her hand on his shoulder, a visible halo of light suffusing both of them as she blessed his aura with a healing calm.

And then suddenly, two old men sat at the table with them, a bottle of shine and five shot glasses in front of them.

'Holy shit,' yelled Griff. 'I hate it when you dudes do that.'

'Shine?' offered mister Reeve.

Griff took the proffered glass with a smile. No matter how shocked you were, one didn't turn down ambrosia.

'We need to talk,' said mister Bolin, addressing Brenner.

'Fuck off,' snarled the wolfman.

Mister Bolin turned to Grandma. 'You have not told him,' he stated.

Grandma shook her head. 'Look at him. It would be too much.'

'What?' growled Brenner.

Grandma gave the Watchers a warning glance, that they both totally ignored.

'Shadow is pregnant with your child,' declared mister Reeve.

Brennerwolf froze. Then he shrank back to his human and sunk down in the chair, like a puppet whose strings had just been cut.

'Hell, dude. Heavy,' breathed Griff. 'I'm sorry, man. Still, not a problem. We'll find her soon. I promise.'

'Where is she?' asked Brenner quietly.

'We don't know,' answered mister Reeve.

'Bullshit. Tell me.'

'We give you our words,' said mister Bolin. 'We know she was taken by the dark lord, or at least by one of his minions. But we know not where she is right now. Her whereabouts are powerfully warded.'

'Why?' asked Brenner.

'We cannot say.'

'Can't or won't?'

'That does not matter,' said mister Bolin.

'He will have taken her to hell,' said Brenner.

'No,' denied mister Reeve. 'The last thing Abaddon would do is hand an excuse for an Authority to enter his realm. The father of lies will not risk a direct confrontation that may escalate.'

'I have already been to hell,' argued Brenner. 'And there was no confrontation. Well, not with the big stink-hole himself.'

'No,' said mister Reeve. 'You have been to a version of hell. Not the home of the defiler. Trust us, Shadow is in some corporeal prison. You need to find where.'

'Obviously,' acknowledged Brenner 'How?'

'Use your followers, your friends, your power.'

'Are you going to help?'

The Watchers sighed in unison. 'It is forbidden,' answered mister Reeve.

'Of course it is,' sneered Brenner. 'Okay then, why don't you both just piss off.'

The two old men frowned. And disappeared.

'You should treat them with more respect,' advised Grandma.

'No,' answered Brenner. 'We need to see Solomon.'

Chapter 7

'I thought you lost all your money,' said Griff.

'I didn't lose it, you nineteen-sixties reprobate,' answered Solomon. 'I spent it to kill all Brenner's enemies. You should remember. You were there, you old half-wit.'

'It took us almost a year to get back on top,' said Suki. 'Barely an inconvenience.'

Griff cast his gaze about the magnificent penthouse, taking in the floor to ceiling view of the Las Vegas strip at night, the Steinway Harmony Grand piano, original Monet and Picasso paintings, and the Mah Jong furniture. The soft furnishings alone came in at over a million dollars.

'Got anything to eat?' asked the old man. 'I'm starving.'

'I've instructed the hotel to send up food,' said Suki. Then she turned to Grandma and bowed deeply. 'Malak,' she greeted. 'You honor us with your presence.'

Grandma smiled.

'Yes,' agreed Solomon. 'Although I must say, I'm surprised to see you here,' he added. 'In a good way, it's just… well, didn't expect to see you here.'

Grandma laughed. 'In sin city, you mean?'

Solomon shrugged.

'I've been here many times before,' informed Grandma. 'Spent a whole month here once back in the day. Stayed with Frank and the boys in the Sands Hotel, before they blew it up and built the Venetian.'

'Wait,' interjected Griff. 'You knew Blue Eyes.'

Grandma nodded.

'You never told me.'

Grandma gave him a wink. 'What happens in Vegas, stays in Vegas.'

'Enough banter,' growled Brenner. 'We gotta get busy.'

'We've already got all of our resources looking for Shadow,' said Suki. 'I got onto it immediately after Grandma phoned to tell us. Private detectives, police departments all over the country, even our contacts in the FBI and the military. The best thing to do now would be to get some rest and wait for information. As soon as we have something to react to, we shall do so.'

'Hey, buddy,' said Griff. 'I know it's hard waiting. But Suki's right. We can't fuck shit up until we know what shit to fuck up.'

Brenner nodded, but said nothing.

'When's that food coming?' reiterated Griff. 'Dude could starve to death here.'

Before anyone could answer, the doorbell chimed and Suki went to open the private elevator.

A small army of servers wheeled out a veritable cornucopia of foods, ranging from sushi and salads to steaming piles of prime rib and fixings.

'Now that's what I'm talking about,' exclaimed Griff.

'Hurry up and eat,' said Grandma. 'Then you and I are going to hit the tables.'

'You gamble?' asked Griff.

'Does the pope shit in the woods?' confirmed Grandma.

Griff chuckled and started loading his plate.

***

Grandma took out her tobacco pouch and loaded her pipe, taking her time to ensure it was well seated before she put it to flame.

'You gonna bet or not?' asked the man sitting opposite her.

'Patience, child,' replied Grandma with a wink. 'Anyway, why you in such a rush to lose your money?'

'What makes you think I'm gonna lose?'

Grandma chuckled. 'Because you bluff like a five-year-old who just broke the cookie jar. I'm all in,' she concluded, pushing the massive pile of chips into the center of the table.

There was a collective gasp from the people watching.

The current pot stood at over three hundred thousand dollars. Grandma had started the evening with eight thousand.

The man flipped his cards one at a time. Two aces. The dealer added another ace.

'Read em and weep,' he chuckled. 'Three bullets.'

Grandma smiled and flipped. A seven of hearts. And a four of diamonds.

'Ha,' crowed the man. 'You got feathers.'

'Count them,' snapped Grandma.

The man stared for a full two seconds then shook his head. 'Son of a bitch. A straight.'

'Oh yeah,' said Griff. 'Come to papa. Griff needs a new pair of shoes.'

But before the old man could grab any chips, Grandma slid them all across the table. 'For the house,' she said. 'You boys and girls have yourselves a party.'

Then she got up and headed for the private elevator.

Griff stared open mouthed at the small fortune left lying on the table. Then someone in the crowd started clapping and was immediately joined by everyone else there.

Griff shook his head and followed his partner from the room.

'Really?' he asked as he caught up.

Grandma winked at him. 'It's just money.'

'But the eight grand stake?'

'As I said, just money. Rich man, camel, eye of the needle and all that.'

Griff sighed.

'Hey, sweetie,' purred Grandma. 'If you want some money, I got loads.'

'You never told me.'

'So, how much you want?'

'None.'

'Exactly.'

The elevator arrived, they got in and both started laughing as it went up to the penthouse.

When they arrived, Grandma got out, then she gave Griff a quick kiss. 'Listen,' she said. 'I've got to go. Things to do. But don't worry, I'll be in touch.'

Griff nodded as the Malak ripped open a tear in time and space and left.

Then he sighed and went to fix himself a stiff whisky.

Chapter 8

The various Quartets had never worked together before. It was the Dark Lord's instructions that they remain separate, each to their own area.

And then Brenner and his associates had destroyed the American Cabal in one fell swoop.

Which put the proverbial fox amongst the chickens.

So now, for the first time ever, The European, Russian, Asian and African Quartets were combining their respective forces and intelligence.

The leaders of each group were currently attending a Zoom conference.

'We are supposed to be hyper-secret dark cabal, not some work-from-home personnel department,' stated the Asian number one. 'So what's with the Zoom. Don't we have our own dark-web meeting room? What next, Twitter accounts for all? Hash-tag, the Darkness cometh.'

One of the European representatives shrugged as he adjusted his camera. 'The thing is, this Zoom thing works really well.'

'So do buses, doesn't mean we should use public transport like peasants.'

'Enough,' interjected the head of the African cabal. 'I call this meeting to order.'

'Who put you in charge?' asked the European number one, a man with an obvious Germanic accent.

'I am the oldest.'

'By a few months.'

'So? You know full well that seniority is everything in our organization. The Dark Lord has proclaimed it so.'

'Okay, fine, whatever.'

The African number one allowed himself a tiny victorious smirk. 'As you know,' he continued. 'The mother of the Messenger is being held captive in a neutral location, until the brat has been birthed and is ready for the ceremony.

'You have all provided a squad of ten of your top warriors and mages. These have been bolstered with a horde of assorted demons and other denizens of darkness to track down the Wolfman and exterminate him, and his associates.

'As well as this, we have brought all of our influence to bear on various government departments, para-military groups, religious cults, and lawmakers throughout the world to join our hunt. The Dark Lord has instructed us to place a sum of one hundred million dollars on the wolfman's head.'

The Russian leader scoffed. 'Obviously I have done all the Master requested. But isn't this a little bit of an overkill?'

The African leader raised an eyebrow. 'This man and his associates managed to exterminate the incredibly powerful American quartet without raising a sweat. He blew up the entire building they were in. An entire building in the middle of Las Vegas. No, this time we will not underestimate him. This time, he is going down.

'And then shall begin the fall of man. With the Messenger out of the picture and the correct sacrifices made, there will be no way the false god and his followers can stand against us.

'All glory to the Dark Lords name.'

'Hail and glory,' intoned the rest of the quartet members.

Chapter 9

Somewhere in America.

A large corrugated iron warehouse.

Nondescript, old but well maintained.

Scattered around it, a series of heavy canvas tents circa 1940's and a large training ground complete with shooting range and outdoor weight training equipment.

In the near distance a mountain with a series of noticable caves. Yellow mist creeps from the caves. The stench of brimstone is redolent in the morning air.

There be demons.

We see inside the warehouse.

The combined warriors of the Quartet stand in rows.

These men comprise the spear of the organization. Not for them the comfort of offices, and Zoom meetings. Of luxury and indulgence.

These were the men the Quartet leaders sent when some serious killing needed to be done.

Europe. Asia. Russia. Africa.

They do not mingle.

The Russian captain is shouting. '*Nyet.* No one person is in charge. We will each run our squads autonomously.'

The German captain scoffed and gave a scornful laugh. 'Don't be ridiculous,' he said. 'Obviously, *we* should be in charge.'

'Well, I want to know why the officers have the same accommodation as the troops,' asked the Nigerian leader of the African squad. 'It is disrespectful to expect leaders to live at the same level as minions. I am less than happy. I demand my own tent.'

'My squad will begin training,' interjected the Asian leader. 'As it is obvious, we shall be doing most of the work in this group.'

Before anyone could respond, a foul wind shivered the building, the door crashed open and in front of them appeared a being.

Ten feet tall, gleaming scarlet skin, small, black leathery wings, eyes of darkest obsidian and a set of swept-back horns on his head.

The Nigerians were the first to prostrate themselves. '*Ogbanje*,' they called out in near unison.

The demon sneered at them all, his red eyed glare slowly driving them all, one by one, to their knees. The final man to genuflect was the Asian captain. A middle-aged man of obvious physical prowess, and even more apparent mental fortitude. A fifth dan black belt in karate, Ju-Jitsu and Kung Fu, he was considered a master of his arts.

Even as he acquiesced, he only dropped his eyes for a brief moment, showing the barest minimum of respect.

'I am the Abysmal Lord, Zobrondo,' roared the demon. '*I* am the leader. There will be no dissention, no discussion and no insubordination. Only obedience.'

The demon lord's announcement was followed by much obsequious groveling.

Zobrondo beckoned to the Asian captain. 'You, stand by me.'

The captain complied.

'What is your name?' asked the demon lord.

'I am captain Yang.'

Zobrondo chuckled. 'You show spirit, captain Yang. Truly remarkable. I have heard of you. They say you are the ultimate warrior.'

Yang nodded slightly. 'Thank you, lord.'

Zobrondo stared at the man for fully twenty seconds. Then he reached forward and touched his forehead with the tip of one of his talons.

Yang's head exploded.

Then his body dropped to the floor and twitched for a short while, taking a while to come to terms with its sudden, horrific demise.

Zobrondo doubled over with laughter.

'Ultimate warrior, my shiny red ass,' he chortled. Then he randomly pointed at another member of the Asian squad. 'You. Name?'

'Specialist Zhao, my lord.'

'Zhao, you are the captain now. Right, everyone, listen up. This is my plan.'

Chapter 10

'Ded, we're doing everything we can,' said Griff. 'Everyone is searching. My guys, Solomons guys, all the shifters. Suki has even sent out representatives to every person you have ever helped. Vast sums of money are been thrown at it. They will find something soon.'

'Not soon enough,' growled Brenner. 'And where's Grandma?'

Griff shrugged. 'Don't know. Says she had stuff to take care of. She'll be back.' He lit a pair of cigarettes and passed one to Brenner. 'Try this. It's one of Solomon's hand-rolled Turkish shit. Cost a fortune, but what the hell, it's only money. Solomon's money.'

Brenner accepted the smoke with a begrudging smile.

'Look, dude,' continued Griff. 'I know you like to work on the, just fuck shit up method of attack, but as I said before, until we find what shit we need to fuck up, there's nothing we can do'.

Brenner took a drag and let it out with a sigh.

As he did so, Suki walked in, an expression of concern on her face.

'Some strange stuff going on here,' she said.

'Explain,' asked Griff.

'Brenner is coming up on the radar everywhere we look. Seriously, whoever we contact seems to know about him. His name echoes through the halls of power. Washington, the military, private contractors. And our contacts are being less than helpful. Not aggressively so, but it's like they're nervous to talk to me. I can't figure out what's going on.'

Give me a few minutes,' said Griff as he took out his cell and started punching in numbers.

Twenty minutes later he finished his third and final call.

'It's bad,' he confirmed. 'Seems there's a hit out on you, big man.'

'How much?'

'A hundred million, US.'

Brenner nodded. 'Acceptable. At least whoever it is, is taking me seriously.'

Suki laughed. 'Really. One hundred million? You call that serious? Hell, Solomon and I lost over six hundred million on your last caper. No ways, one hundred is child's play.'

'Still, it's gonna get a lot of kids into the sandpit,' noted Griff. 'We going to be fighting off uglies twenty-four-seven.'

'I'll keep digging,' said Suki as she left the room.

'Dude,' said Griff. 'I don't want to be *that* guy, but the last time you created a ruckus even one tenth as much as this, pretty much every man and his dog tried to kill you. Maybe we should lay low for a bit. At least until we know what's going on.'

'Let them come,' growled Brenner. 'All the more people to question regarding Shadow.'

Griff grimaced and then nodded. 'Whatever, Ded. I'm with you.'

Chapter 11

'Listen up, people, this is a grade A, fur lined, ocean going, cock up of epic proportions.'

Charles Miller glowered at the assembled agents with what he assumed to be a steely-eyed glare. He actually looked more like a man who had forgotten his contact lenses and was attempting to squint the audience into focus.

The highly polished table in the windowless underground room was easily large enough to entertain the twenty-seven men-in-black sitting around it. It was a nod to the true misogyny and the entrenched old-boy network of all present that not a single female was seated there.

'This is priority Alpha-alpha-alpha,' continued Miller. 'Eyes only, from the very top.'

He depressed the button on his remote and a slide machine whirred into life, projecting a six-by-six-foot picture onto the screen.

'Slides,' commented one of the suits. 'Holy shit-nuts. What are we, back in the damn eighties? You don't got PowerPoint and a projector?'

'Shut up, Johnson,' snapped Miller. 'This is old school info.'

'You can't get someone to transfer it? Jesus H Christ, Charles, this department has a bigger budget than the gross national product of Sweden.'

Miller scowled and pointed at the blurry image. 'This is the man we're looking for.'

'That photo is like sixty years old,' interjected Johnson. 'Hell, he's wearing Vietnam camo. Haven't you got anything more recent?'

'No.'

'Well can't the tech boys do some computer enhancement?' continued Johnson. 'At least give us a mockup of what he might look like now.'

Miller frowned, and it was clear he was perturbed. And more than a little puzzled. 'The higher ups tell me … this is what he looks like.'

'Now?'

Miller nodded. 'Yeah. Not sure how that works. But apparently, he looks identical to this sixty-year-old image. Maybe longer hair and rough shaven. But essentially, that's him.'

'He got a name?' asked another one of the other suits.

'Brenner. Sergeant Ded Brenner.'

'Dead?' repeated the suit.

'Yep.'

'Weird name.'

'Whatever,' continued Miller as he flicked to the next slide.

'Ah, shit,' he exclaimed. 'Someone put this in upside-down. Hold on.' He spent a minute pushing various buttons, turning the antiquated machine on and off, and eventually got the slide right-side-up.

'There. The next person of interest is this. Solomon Hopewell.'

'Oh, come on,' exclaimed Johnson. 'Seriously, Charles? That's totally out of focus. What good is that? Got any that we can actually see the guy's features?'

Miller looked embarrassed. 'No. Apparently, it's impossible to photograph this guy. No one knows why. But that's as good as it gets.'

The projector cycled again, bringing up a photo of Griff, circa 1960's. Camo, carrying an M16, Lucky Strike dangling from his mouth.

'Don't tell me,' said Johnson. 'This guy also still looks the same.'

Miller shook his head. 'No. Well, to be honest, we aren't one hundred percent sure about that. Rumors differ. He got older, but then some say, he got younger again. Anyway, these men are top of our shit list, gentlemen. We need to find them and take them out with extreme prejudice.'

No one spoke for a full minute.

Finally, one of the suits that hadn't spoken yet raised his hand.

'Just speak, Carlton,' snapped Miller. 'This isn't a godsdamn school room.'

'Umm … it's just that, when I was with Homeland Security, I think I heard of these guys. Well, I heard of an operation that allegedly involved them.'

'So?'

'Everyone involved died. I mean everyone. Private contractors. Black Ops companies. Navy Seals. Everyone.'

'Just rumors, Carlton,' said Miller. 'Now I need you all to put together a plan of action. This needs to happen, and it needs to happen now.'

Again, no one spoke for a while.

Then Johnson said. 'Charles?'

'Yes.'

'What the actual hell is really going on?'

Chapter 12

Colonel Colby Hislop.

CEO of Outsource International.

The bland corporate exterior of the twelve-story building in upper Manhattan belied the company's actual purpose.

Outsource International was nothing less than a PMC. A private military company.

The colonel's corner office housed a massive desk, a wet bar, a permanent massage table, a dining table and a slew of leather wingbacks.

Hislop sat at his desk, hands steepled in front of him, face expressionless.

Opposite him sat four more men.

Whereas it could be extrapolated from his general demeanor that Hislop was once a warrior, even though he had allowed the lines to blur. There was no such hesitation in pigeonholing the other four men.

They were younger, leaner, and all sported the thousand-yard-stare of the front-line soldier.

All Americans.

All professionals.

Once they were soldiers. But are now they were more like … problem solvers.

In that they removed other people's problems.

Hislop slid four dossiers across the desk.

The men read them. Silently. Thoroughly.

In approximately eleven minutes they all put the dossiers down at the same time.

'Questions?' asked Hislop.

'Yeah, what gives, boss?'

'Meaning?'

'Some old dude. A guy with no known photos. Another dude last seen in the sixties, and what looks like an Indian supermodel. Little known about any of them, apart from the obvious fact that someone with loads of pull wants them all dead.'

'Yeah,' agreed Hislop. 'It's all a bit sketchy. Particularly the info I've managed to get on that Sergeant Hopewell guy. The one who we can't photograph. One of my contacts assures me he was part of some super-secret, ultra-violent black ops gig that involved some real dark shit. Proper Island of Doctor Moreau stuff, human-animal hybrids, genetic splicing, proper nightmare material.'

'I've also heard some serious scuttlebutt regarding that Brenner guy,' interjected one of the hard men.

'What sort of stuff?' asked Hislop.

The man shrugged. 'Hard to say. Clearly mainly bullshit, but suffice to say – not a guy to be messed with.'

Hislop sighed. 'Okay, there's more to this than meets the eye. However, the amount of money being offered is beyond obscene. So, we're doing it. We're going to make these problems go away.'

The hard men nodded. They were there to make money. And the fact that this mission may be a little more difficult than most was reflected in the fiscal renumeration.

It was time to rock and roll.

Chapter 13

In as much as a demon Lord could look frustrated, Zobrondo did.

His lieutenant, Farnet, stood next to him, a homogenous amalgamation of far too many arms and legs and claws and teeth.

'They obviously fear me,' mused the demon lord. 'Yet still they resist my orders.'

'Yes,' agreed Farnet. 'They fear.'

'But when I order them to work together, they do not.'

Farnet shrugged, an altogether unpleasant sight considering his preponderance of shoulders. 'They are currently doing as you commanded, my lord.'

Zobrondo shook his head. 'No. Humans are very deceitful. They only appear to be working together. But they hate each other. The African cabal will barely glance at the Asians. And as for the Europeans, they consider themselves superior to all of the other groups. I believe humans call this, working to the letter of the law. They are ostensibly doing as I command, but underneath, they are doing their utmost to disobey. Quite admirable in some way.'

'Perhaps you should let them operate autonomously, my lord.'

'They will be no match for the Authority. Nor the vampire,' scoffed Zobrondo. 'Even combined and working together they will find it no easy task.'

'I agree, my lord. However, they are too arrogant to comprehend that.'

Zobrondo laughed. 'True, good lieutenant. Perhaps they need taking down a peg or three. Do we know where the wolfman is right now?'

'We suspect he is in Las Vegas.'

'Ah, what a perfect town,' sighed Zobrondo. 'The closest the humans have to true debauchery. I think I shall allow the Europeans to have a go. They suffer from the most misguided sense of superiority. Brief them, lieutenant, and then send them on their way.'

Farnet bowed low. 'As you command, my lord, so shall it be.'

Chapter 14

Member of the Vatican Swiss Guard, Sergeant Maximillian Keller, had been summoned by various Cardinals before. Sometimes to discuss plans for the Holy Father's security, and sometimes to ask him to look into sundry ecclesiastical members backgrounds.

But since he had been ordained as a Knight of the Holy See, the military arm of the Vatican's paranormal investigation unit, he had been summoned more and more to seek out and destroy denizens of evil.

Vampires, ghouls, the possessed, and even demons.

In all that time, however, he had never actually met the Holy Father himself.

Papa.

The Pope.

Servant of God John Paul II

Until now.

'Rise, my son,' intoned the Pope.

Max stood up; the feeling of the medal the Holy Father had just placed around his neck felt much heavier than the mere single ounce it actually weighed.

The church had just bestowed upon him, the Sovereign Military Order of Malta. An honor only given thus far to three members of the church ever.

The other two had died on the next mission they had taken part in. A sort of pre-posthumous, posthumous award.

Then Papa tasked him with his next assignment

'You must travel to America,' he had informed him. 'And there you will find a certain Ded Brenner. Present yourself to him and inform him the Holy Catholic Church has sent you to help him in his quest.'

Max bowed. 'It shall be done, Father.'

The Pope smiled, then he blessed the young knight.

'Ego facultáte mihi ab Apostólica Sede tribúta, indulgéntiam plenáriam et remissiónem ómnium peccatórum tibi concédo, in nómine Patris, et Fílii, et Spíritus Sancti. Amen.'

'By the authority which the Apostolic See has given me, I grant you a full pardon and the remission of all your sins in the name of the Father, and of the Son, and of the Holy Spirit.'

Maximillian smiled as his suspicions were realized. The Father had granted him absolution. They did not expect him to survive this mission.

'I am not coming back?' he questioned the Father.

John Paul shook his head. 'I very much doubt it, my son.'

'Will anyone else accompany me?'

Again, the pope shook his head. 'This is something only you can do. I have been informed by the highest authority,' he continued, glancing heavenward.

Max smiled. 'Thank you for the honor, Papa.'

He bowed once more and then left the room, following the Cardinal Angelo Sandri to his briefing.

What he was next told, left him both humbled and afraid.

For the Catholic church knew much more about Brenner and his associates than any other organization on the planet.

And now Maximillian Keller knew he had been tasked with helping to save the earth from a veritable apocalypse.

Chapter 15

The Falcon 900 jet landed at the private airstrip some twenty miles from Las Vegas.

The dozen members of the European squad disembarked, and proceeded to unload their equipment from the hold and transfer it into the small convoy of waiting vehicles.

Zobrondo had not sent any demon overwatch with them, allowing the team full control over how they handled their mission.

The Europeans had seen this as proof of their superiority over the other lesser squads. Their captain, Gunter Felsen, ex-

German military, had gone as far as to refer to the other teams as *Untermensch*, people considered both socially and racially inferior.

It took them a little over an hour to transfer their equipment, which included numerous firearms, explosives, various squad support weapons, ammunition, body armor and uniforms.

As soon as they were finished, the convoy set off to the rented temporary headquarters.

***

Suki strode into the room. 'Just been contacted by one of our assets,' she announced as she threw a handful of photos onto the coffee table.

'Chartered jet just dropped these jokers off at a private airfield North of here. They weren't even trying to keep a low profile. Unloaded a shithouse full of ordnance and then drove to that place there,' she pointed at one of the photos. 'The address is on the back.'

Solomon scowled at the picture of the house while Griff and Brenner flicked through the photos of the personnel.

'Hey, I know this guy,' stated Griff. 'German dude, Gunter something or other. Ex KSK, German special forces. Fell off the grid a few years back. Some say he joined a religious cult. Loads of rumors. But whatever, the guy is good. Real good. Do we know why they're here?'

Solomon scoffed. 'They're here for Ded, obviously.'

'Not necessarily,' argued Griff.

Everyone stared at him.

Griff shrugged. 'Yeah, true. Sorry, when things go South to this extent, it's always the big man's fault.'

'Push off,' mumbled Brenner. 'I resent that.'

'Do you deny it?' asked Griff.

'No, just resent it.'

'What now?' asked Griff.

'They're here for me,' answered Brenner. 'Let's give them what they want. You know where this place is?'

Solomon nodded. 'And it's sundown in just over an hour, so I'm in.'

Griff laughed. 'Time to fuck shit up?' he questioned.

Brenner nodded. 'It's time.'

Chapter 16

The residence was a sprawling standalone bungalow that had been extended on an ad hoc basis over the last ten years or so. A large, run-down stable block and a series of ramshackle paddocks testified to the fact that at some stage in the past it had probably been some sort of dude ranch or similar.

There was a perimeter fencing, but like the paddocks it was in a state of ill-repair.

There were no guards. No exterior security lights and no CCTV cameras.

Team Brenner had parked their SUV two miles away and humped to the target.

Griff had used the big man as a pack-mule and had him carry an assortment of heavy weaponry, while Griff carried his usual M16 and a few extra magazines.

Neither Brenner or Solomon had bothered to tool up. The plan was to get closeup and personal with the occupants.

Brenner had questions to ask.

'I don't get it,' mumbled Griff as he scoped the house out through a pair of binoculars. 'These guys are acting like complete idiots. And I know Gunter isn't an idiot. What gives? No sentries, no surveillance, no nothing.'

'Hubris,' answered Solomon. 'Most likely been kicking ass for so long he can't even comprehend anyone actually coming after him. In his mind, he's the man to be scared of. Also, German. Arrogant assholes.'

'You can't just say that a whole nation is arrogant,' said Griff.

'Just did,' denied Solomon. 'I fought them in two World Wars on the trot. Damned compulsive invaders. Arrogant.'

Griff shrugged. 'Yeah, suppose you could be right. About the hubris, not necessarily about the Germans on the whole.'

'Doesn't matter why,' interjected Brenner. 'Doesn't change the plan. We go in hot and heavy, fuck their shit up, keep a couple alive to question.'

Griff nodded his agreement. 'Let's get closer,' he said. 'Then we can set up the M240 so I can provide some overwatch. Then you dudes get close and I'll hit the front door with the RPG to provide some shock and awe and get you ingress. After that, it's up to you.'

The team moved closer and set the machinegun up. Then Brenner handed Griff the RPG.

'Have fun,' quipped Griff as Brenner and Solomon moved towards the house, instantly blending into the darkness as if invisible.

Griff gave them a count of twenty, then he lined the sights up on the front door, depressed the trigger and launched the rocket.

Unlike the movies, when one fires an RPG, it does not make a sound like a bottle rocket followed by a polite bang. It's more like the sound of a jet engine taking off followed by an earth-shattering explosion as over two pounds of explosive detonates on impact.

This is followed by a wave of overpressure that will damage any human being within thirty feet.

In short, if you are anywhere near said ordnance's point of impact, it will surely mess up your day.

Before the resultant fireball had settled, Brenner and Solomon entered the house, moving so fast as to be a mere blur in the night.

'Go left,' ordered Brenner as he turned right, morphing into his wolfman mode.

Solomon hurtled down the corridor, senses on high alert, fangs and talons ready to slash and tear.

The sound of running footsteps and cussing in various European languages sounded out as the Quartet warriors grabbed weapons and ran to see what the hell was happening.

The European team was comprised of a very specific type of person. Not only were the very best at what they did – murder, mayhem and destruction, they also worshipped the Darkness and reveled in spreading the word of Evil to all.

All supernaturally empowered by their Dark Lord, fanatical, highly trained, full of confidence in their own abilities, and utterly motivated.

As a result, one would expect them to do some serious damage. Even to two paranormal beings like Brenner and Solomon.

Unfortunately, they were like literal babes in the woods. Stomping mewling toddlers carrying guns and mouthing obscenities at their betters.

The entire encounter was over in just under nineteen seconds. If you counted the first explosion as the start of the clock.

Brenner strolled back to the entrance. The walls of the various rooms he had gone through were painted with blood and gore. Dismembered body parts lay scattered about like an explosion in a mortuary.

Blood dripped thickly from his claws, his maw and his fur.

Solomon was still immaculate. Not even a drop of red on his hand-crafted suit. He stared at Brenner and shook his head. 'Gods, you are a messy eater.'

'Didn't eat anyone,' denied Brenner with a growl.

'Chap, you have to work on your technique,' continued Solomon. 'Is it really necessary to act like a living woodchipper with every single body you come across?' He pointed at a sundry piece of flesh that may or may not have been part of a leg. Or arm. 'I mean, what even is that?'

Brenner looked closely and sniffed. 'Shoulder. I think.'

Griff strode into the entrance, his M16 at the ready. He glanced around. 'Wow, Ded, like your work.' Then he looked at Solomon. 'Did you even get involved?'

'Of course I did. Got three of them. Just didn't see the need to spray-paint the entire house with their innards. And I managed to keep two alive, unlike this overpowered angry idiot.'

Brenner shuffled his feet and had the good grace to look embarrassed. 'Yeah, thanks. I did go a bit mental. Just real pissed, you know. The whole Shadow thing.'

'Well, follow uncle Solomon and he shall let you question the survivors.'

Griff and Brenner stalked after the vampire as he led them back to one of the bedrooms. Lying on the floor, thoroughly tied up with bedsheets, were two men. They were both bleeding from multiple cuts on both body and face.

Brennerwolf walked up to the first one and tore his binding off, then he lifted him up. 'What is your name?' he growled.

'Fuck you,' replied the man in a thick Italian accent. Obviously not intimidated by the wolfman's frightening visage.

Brenner didn't even hesitate as he shattered the man's right arm with a simple turn of his wrist. The man grunted in agony, but still didn't answer.

Brenner grasped the man's nose, and ripped it off. Blood sprayed across the room as he screamed in agony.

'Dude,' exclaimed Griff. 'Slow down.'

Brenner removed one of the man's ears, jerking it off with a savage tug.

'Gino,' yelled the man. 'Gino De Campo.'

'Where is Shadow?'

The man looked genuinely baffled. 'Who?'

'I'm not going to ask again.'

'I don't know, I swear,' screamed the man.

'Then you are of no use to me,' breathed the wolfman. And with terrifying slowness, he tore the man's arms off. Finally, he snapped his neck, dropped him and removed the second man's bindings as he picked him up.

'Name?' asked Brenner.

The man stared at him, but didn't answer.

'That's Gunter,' interjected Griff. The Kraut I told you about. You ain't gonna get him to talk.'

'Ded,' said Solomon softly. 'Let me question this one. Seriously. Trust me.'

'I am not afraid of you, dog boy,' sneered Gunter. 'Nor you, vampire.'

'Well then you are a very stupid man,' said Solomon as he grasped the German by his face and looked into his eyes. 'Talk to me,' continued the man in black. 'Who sent you?'

'Ha, there is no secret to that,' answered Gunter. 'We are the warrior arm of the European Quartet. Our leader sent us.'

'Oh, the Eurotrash-version of those asswipes we took down when you blew up that hotel,' noted Griff. 'Must say, I'd heard there were more of the asswipes. Just wasn't sure until now. How many more Quartets are there?'

'Many more,' raved Gunter. 'And they will find you and kill you all.'

'They'll need to be a lot better than you dickheads,' scoffed Griff. 'Because frankly, you were pathetic. Seriously, it was embarrassing.'

'Where is Shadow,' roared Brenner.

Gunter stared at him, but before he could respond, his entire body began to shake like he was having a fit. His tongue bulged from his mouth as his head flicked back and forth, and blood poured from his ears. Then without warning, both of his eyes exploded.

Solomon ducked to the side and dropped him so quickly, he still had not a mark on him.

'What the hell?' yelled Brenner. 'He's dead.'

'Some bad Juju,' said Griff.

Solomon nodded in agreement. 'Yep, that is some next level curse or something right there. Fellow couldn't even think of telling us anything and his head popped.'

'Shit,' howled Brenner. 'Shit, shit, shit.'

'Calm down, big man,' urged Solomon. 'Let's go through this place with a fine-tooth comb, see if we can gather any intel.'

Brenner took a deep breath and nodded.

***

'I am not sure any of you have seen this before,' said Zobrondo. 'It is a power that servants of the Dark Lord are oft gifted with. Some call it a scrying wall, others a seeing slab. Suffice to say, it is a magical representation of an area and a time that has been prepared for the projection of said spelling.'

The demon lord checked to see the collected Quartet warriors were keeping up, but a single glance revealed he had left quite a few behind. Gifted at fighting they were, but in the intelligence stakes, not the sharpest tools in the box.

'It's like CCTV,' he added and saw the light of understanding dawn on them. 'Now, behold. Witness the vaunted European team's mission.'

The wall lit up like a high-definition TV, except for the oddly disported image, as if the scene was being viewed through a fisheye lens.

They saw the door explode in a ball of fire. The audio not as high a quality as the visual, but still loud enough to vibrate the room they were in.

Two attackers moved through the dying flames, so fast it was impossible to make out any detail.

The vision split into two separate screens. One followed what appeared to be a massive humanoid wolf.

The other tracked a pale faced man in a black suit.

The next handful of seconds were filled with such overt violence that even the hardened minions of evil watching were shaken.

A minute later they watched in horror as the wolfman literally tore Gino limb from limb.

Then Gunter's eyes exploded.

Fade to black.

No one spoke for a few seconds.

Eventually, Ivan Fedorov, the Russian captain said. 'Holy shit.'

'I agree,' answered Zobrondo. 'Now, gentlemen, do you think you can put aside your petty human differences and concentrate on your given task. For as I have already told you, this target will not be easy to overcome. Not at all.'

There was a general murmur of agreement as the warriors' previous view of their place on the totem pole shifted down a few notches.

It was time to get their act together, or die.

Chapter 17

'That was a bust,' said Brenner.

'Not completely,' disagreed Griff. 'We know there are more of those Quartet dudes. We know they gonna keep sending people after you, and we sorta know that they not very good at what they do.'

'Yeah well, you just explained pretty much everyone who's been trying to off me for the past fifty years. I ain't short of enemies. But we still got no closer to where Shadow is.'

'Hey,' interjected Solomon. 'They keep sending people after you, we keep getting to ask more questions. Eventually we'll get someone to talk.'

The drove in silence for another twenty minutes, approaching the outskirts of Vegas.

'Looks like we might have incoming,' noted Griff as he glanced in the rearview mirror.

Solomon swiveled in his seat and scoped out their rear. 'Three black SUV's,' he said, his perfect night-vison able to pick out every detail. 'Five men per car. Dressed in a mix of combat gear. Automatic weapons. Coming in fast.'

'Pedal to the metal, Griff,' said Brenner. 'Let's see what happens.'

Griff hit the accelerator. 'Hey, Solomon,' he asked. 'This SUV bulletproof?'

'Within reason.'

'What's that mean?'

'Run flat tires. Polycarbonate windows, and Kevlar in the doors. Should be fine for handguns and maybe 5.56mm. Anything heavier, we got problems.'

'What those boys carrying?' asked Brenner.

'Hey, I have good eyesight, I'm not omniscient,' snapped Solomon.

'Whatever, guess.'

'Different weapons. All foreign. Small. No worries, unless they also got RPG's or shit.'

'Sounds like private contractors,' said Brenner. 'Undoubtably, they'll have some heavy stuff with them.'

There was a muzzle-flash from one of the followers and a couple of slugs hit the rear windshield, leaving small pockmarks in the polycarbonate.

That was followed by a longer burst that hammered more rounds into the back of the SUV, but caused little to no effect.

'Should I return fire?' asked Brenner.

'Not yet,' answered Griff. 'I'm turning onto the freeway. Let's see if I can lose them.'

The engine note pitched higher as Griff lay a heavy foot on the accelerator. The SUV began to pull away, but not at any appreciable speed.

A few more slugs hit the rear windshield again.

'Give it up, dudes,' yelled Griff. 'It's the definition of insanity to keep doing the same thing over and over and expect a different result.'

'They can't hear you,' quipped Solomon.

'I know,' admitted Griff. 'Looks like they don't care much about collateral damage. Could easy hit someone else.'

The SUV sped towards the strip, fast approaching the famous, 'Welcome to Las Vegas' sign.

'Hey, looks like they're bringing out the heavy stuff,' warned Solomon as he glanced back at their attackers. 'RPG.'

'They'll never hit us with that,' scoffed Brenner.

There was an explosion of light followed closely by the shriek of the rocket propelled grenade being launched.

As Brenner had predicted, the missile careened well overhead, missing them by yards.

It did not, however, miss the famous sign.

With a thunderous detonation, the sign disappeared in a ball of flame.

'What the hell,' shouted Solomon with an unusual display of emotion. 'Nobody shoots up signs in my town. Particularly that one.' He leaned over the back seat and grabbed the M240 machine gun, his superhuman strength allowing him to lift it with ease. 'Griff, open the sunroof,' he commanded as he looped the two hundred and fifty round belt over his shoulder.

The sunroof slid back.

Solomon stood up on the back seat and brought the machinegun to bear. Even though the SUV was travelling at over a hundred miles an hour, and Griff was weaving from side to side to avoid the traffic, Solomon's supernatural abilities allowed him to stand as still as if he were on a gimbal.

The vampire gave the leading attacker a full three second burst, aiming for the windshield.

All thirty of the 7.62x51mm rounds struck true, completely removing the windshield, tearing the through the occupants and killing all five of them. Their SUV careened off the freeway, crashing through the barriers, flipping as it did, and landing on its back in the middle of Dean Martin Drive.

Before Solomon could turn to the next attacker, Griff yanked the wheel and exited onto Frank Sinatra Drive.

'Hey,' yelled Solomon. 'I was busy. Why did you leave the freeway?'

'Not happy with all this firefighting and the possibility for collateral damage,' answered Griff. 'What if you miss and take out a car with some kiddies in it?'

'I don't miss,' argued the man in black.

'Everybody misses at some stage.'

'Not me. Anyway, they're still following us.'

'Persistent mother humpers, aren't they,' noted Brenner. 'We need to try and take a few alive so we can have a conversation.'

'Sure,' quipped Griff. 'First though, let's just try to not get fragged.'

Solomon stood up again, but couldn't get a bead on either of their followers. There were too many cars between them, and both they and Griff were weaving about.

The sound of multiple police sirens filled the air as every cop in Vegas descended on the remains of the sign.

'Go that way,' said Solomon. 'Towards the Harry Reid Airport. There's a lot of empty spaces, parking lots, shit like that. Less people. We can take them out there.'

Griff followed his instructions and gunned the SUV forward, pushing it to the very edge of its capabilities.

Solomon pointed again. 'There, take a sharp right, it leads to a building site. The foundations are in place, and there's a load of outbuildings and scaffolding. It's a good killing ground.'

Brenner scoped out the area as Griff drove in, smashing through a pair of chain-link gates. 'Take us as close as you can to the side of that warehouse,' he instructed. 'I'm going to jump out of the sunroof and get on the top of that building. Then I can ambush one of the vehicles. Solomon, I'll take the rear one, can you shoot the crap outa the other one?'

Sure,' affirmed the man in black. 'No bystanders here.'

Griff steered the speeding SUV up alongside the warehouse. Brenner leaped from his seat, changing into his wolfman form as he did.

It was like a high-end magic trick. One moment he was in the car, the next he had disappeared, leaving behind the shredded remains of his t-shirt, jeans and boots.

The two enemy vehicles came screeching into the building site, men hanging out of the windows and firing as they came.

Griff glanced in his rearview mirror and saw Brennerwolf launch himself from the roof of the warehouse and land on top of the second SUV. Then he saw his friend literally tear the vehicle's roof off and jump inside.

Solomon opened up. This time he didn't limit himself to a single three second burst. Instead, he held the trigger down until the rest of the two hundred and fifty round belt was expended.

Griff slowed down and did a tight u-turn. The car Solomon had fired at was a complete wreck. No windows, the engine a mere pile of steaming scrap, the front of the roof had been sawn off from the quantity of high-velocity lead, and every tire had been shredded.

As they drove past it, they could see the bodies inside were chopped to pieces.

'Man, you went a bit overboard, dude,' muttered Griff.

'Yeah well, they broke my sign.'

Brenner, still in wolfman form, was standing outside the second SUV. Two men lay face down on the ground in front of him. Griff stopped the vehicle and he and Solomon got out. Peering into the SUV he noted the other three occupants were dead. And in much the same state as Solomon's kills. Basically, shredded.

'Nice moves,' said Griff.

Brennerwolf growled and the two men on the ground both squeezed their eyes shut at the sound.

'Well, gentlemen,' continued Griff as he lit a cigarette. 'This didn't turn out the way you planned.'

'No shit,' agreed the one attacker.

'So, who sent you?' continued Griff.

'The boss,' answered the same man. 'Colonel Colby Hislop. CEO of Outsource International.'

'Private contractors,' noted Griff. 'And who paid the boss?'

'I don't know. Seriously, if I did, I'd tell you. I don't get paid enough for this shit. I mean, what the hell is this thing?' he used his head to gesture towards Brenner. 'And how the hell can a single man shoot a heavy machine gun from the back of a moving vehicle and not miss?'

'Told you I don't miss,' quipped Solomon.

Griff was about to answer when Brenner leaned down and picked the man up by his neck. He held him in front of his face, feet dangling above the ground. 'Where is Shadow?'

'What?' squealed the man, his face a mask of horror.

'Shadow,' roared Brenner.

'I don't know what you're talking about,' croaked the man.

'Oh, dude,' said Griff. 'That is not going to go down well.'

Brenner stared at the man for a second, and with a flick of his wrist, he snapped his neck.

Then he picked up the next man.

'Shadow?'

The man started to shake violently and the smell of urine filled the air as terror canceled out all of his autonomic biological functions.

'Fuck this,' growled Brenner as he broke the second man's neck and dropped him to the floor.

Griff looked like he was about to say something, but Solomon caught his eye and subtly shook his head. Now was not the time.

Griff nodded in acknowledgment.

The man in black took out his cell and pushed a button. Suki answered within seconds.

'We got problems,' informed Solomon. 'Some bunch of private contractors tried to ice us on the way back from our hit, looks like every man and his dog knows where we are right now.'

'I agree,' answered Suki. 'In fact, there's a gentleman with me at the moment. He arrived an hour ago, came straight to the penthouse and asked to see Brenner, by name.'

Solomon took a short time to think. 'Okay, we need to get out of Vegas. Can you meet us at the Ranch, leave as soon as you can? Maybe you should just kill the stranger.'

'No,' disagreed Suki. 'I think he's on our side. He's wearing a priest's collar. And I get a good feeling about him.'

'I trust your instincts,' said Solomon. 'See you at the Ranch.'

He hung up.

Chapter 18

The Ranch lay approximately fifty miles south of Vegas, just inside the Mojave National Preserve.

Solomon guided Griff through the seemingly featureless landscape. There were no roads, not even tracks to follow.

After grinding through the rocky terrain for over an hour, they came across a fold hidden between a couple of mountains.

Solomon pointed downwards. 'There.'

Griff strained his eyes in the dark, but couldn't see anything, even though the SUV was fitted with upgraded lighting.

'Just keep going straight on,' said Brenner, who had already picked out their destination.

The old man inched forwards until suddenly he saw it.

The building was partly buried, perhaps only two feet standing above the ground. A ramp gave access to a huge steel roller door, but the ramp itself was constructed to look like a natural fissure in the ground.

The roof was covered with rock and dirt, and there were no visible fences or outside power sources.

As they approached, Solomon took out his cell and used it to open the door.

It rolled up silently and Griff drove in.

'Welcome to The Ranch,' said Solomon. 'Hopefully, Suki should be here soon. Let me show you around.'

Chapter 19

Grandma sat opposite the two old men.

Neither of them offered her a shot of shine.

Which was telling. Because the Watchers always offered up their ambrosia.

No one spoke.

Grandma's hair flowed about her like it was a living thing. From her eyes, an unnatural glow suffused the room. And all about her, a halo of light turned her very presence into a thing of ethereal loveliness.

But that was nothing compared to her physical beauty.

Grandma had dropped any semblance of humanity and was now so perfect to look upon as to be transcendent.

She truly looked like the angel she was.

'How did you find us?' asked mister Reeve.

'I have my ways.'

'We are untraceable,' continued mister Reeve. 'We Watch, but remain unseen to all.'

'Not all,' answered Grandma, fluttering her impossible long eyelashes at the ancient Watcher. 'Tell me,' she continued. 'When did manners go out of style?'

Mister Reeve stared at her, uncomprehending.

Mister Bolin saved the moment by filling a shot glass and sliding it over to her. 'Shine?'

Grandma smiled. 'Why, thank you, mister Bolin, it appears there are still some gentlemen in the world.' She tossed it down and held out the glass for a refill.

Mister Bolin complied.

'You have to find her,' she stated.

'We can't,' denied mister Reeve.

Grandma leaned forward, and the light in her eyes changed. The golden glow morphing into a fiery red. 'Listen you mother fuckers,' she growled. 'I'm calling in my favor.'

'We don't owe you a favor,' said mister Reeve.

'Strictly speaking, that's not true. And you know that. But, if that is how you would like to play it, fine, then I shall owe you one. Find her, I know you can.'

Mister Bolin shook his head. It's part of the Great Plan,' he said. 'We may not agree, but His ways are often ineffable.'

'Fuck the Great Plan,' snapped Grandma.

Neither of the Watchers commented on the Malak's blasphemous utterance.

Finally, mister Reeve spoke. 'We shall see what we can do,' he said quietly. 'Within the rules, of course.'

Grandma shook her head. 'Fucking pussies. Well, don't think I am going to stand meekly by while it is within my power to help.'

And in a coruscation of light, she portaled away.

Chapter 20

Rianne, the mother collective of the Poughkeepsie Alpaca Farm, knew there were rules laid down by the powers that be.

Particularly when it came to the Great Plan.

And she knew that these rules were intractable.

But she also knew that some rules were meant to be broken. Or at very least bent to a point just before destruction.

She knew that because an angel had just informed her.

And that very angel sat across the table, her very presence a balm to Rianne's soul.

'But, Grandma,' said Rianne. 'I don't understand. You say the rules cannot be broken, yet surely…'

'Exactly,' interrupted Grandma. 'And the rules state that Brenner shall be responsible for destroying the enemy. All we are doing is ensuring he does as he is destined to do.'

Rianne still looked a little doubtful. 'With all due respect,' she said. 'Your argument seems a bit specious.'

Grandma laughed. 'Yep,' she agreed. 'And that is because it is. But if there is one thing I do know, my child, it is the fact we have free will. The boss is very big on that. And, when it comes down to it, does it seem to you anything I have suggested is evil in any way, shape or form?'

'Tell me again,' insisted Rianne.

'It isn't pertinent to tell you the intricacies of the Great Plan,' said Grandma. 'But as to what we can do to help Brenner, this is *my* great plan.

'I will use my powers to create a perfect simulacrum of Brenner. It shall be a copy of him down to the very last molecule. Even his aura will be indistinguishable from the real thing.

'After that I will cloak one of your girls in Brenner's form. Then we shall spread the joy. Send her, with reinforcements, far and wide. Those ass-monkeys are going to start getting reports of Brenner from all over the country. Let's see how they handle that.'

***

A day later, Grandma, Rianne and Greta stood in the small hall together.

'It's uncanny,' said Rianne, her voice hushed in awe.

Before them stood Brenner. Well, obviously not Ded himself, but a perfect, breathing replica of him.

'Can it speak?' asked Greta, the leader of the *Kriegshexen*. The combat arm of the hedge witch community.

'No,' admitted Grandma. 'But then neither does he. Much.'

The two witches nodded in agreement. Brenner was known for many things, but garrulous verbosity was definitely not one of them.

'Now,' continued Grandma. 'The final step. We lay the image over you.'

'Is this going to hurt?' asked Greta.

Grandma shook her head. Then, she took the combat witch by the hand and began to chant, while walking her towards Brenner's image. And slowly, Greta and Brenner morphed together, melting and reforming until finally, only Brenner was there.

He/she looked down at himself, studying his own body.

'This is crazy,' said Brenner in Greta's voice. 'Oops, mustn't forget,' she/he continued. 'Don't talk.'

'Come outside,' said Grandma.

Brenner-Greta followed the Malak outside.

There was a close replica of Brenner's Harley. A matt black ratbike that was once a purebred, but was now an amalgam of whatever worked best.

It was not exactly the same, but to anyone who did not know him intimately, it was close enough.

Greta climbed on board and fired it up. Then she turned, looked at them and grinned.

'Holy shit,' exclaimed Grandma. 'It's perfect. Right,' she continued. 'Get the rest of the *Kriegshexen* mounted up on the other Harleys we got, and send them out there. Tell them to make a noise, be seen. And if anyone attacks them, vengeance be mine. And by that, I mean yours.'

Rianne smiled. 'I shall make it so, Grandma.'

'Good. Now I got to be moving along. Next stop, Shadow's clan. I think I'm going to lay a simulacrum onto Rufus 'Fucking' Johnstone.'

Rianne raised an eyebrow. 'Strange name, why do the call him that?'

Grandma simply grinned and then tore a hole in time and space and left.

Chapter 20

'No fucking way,' yelled Rufus. 'What if I can't fucking change back. I don't wanna be that wolf-brained, sad mother fucker for the rest of whatever. Fuck that, for fucks sake.'

Grandma laughed, and the hallowed light about her pulsed in time.

'I should have fucking known something fucked up was going on when some rando pitched up with a shitty black ratbike that looked like Brenner's,' continued Rufus. 'But this, turning me into the wolfman, not in my wildest fucking dreams.'

Grandma waited while Rufus 'Fucking' Johnston continued raving. Eventually, even he ran out of things to swear about.

'Finished?' asked Grandma.

Rufus shrugged.

'You know you have to do it? Ded needs your help.'

Rufus sighed. 'Will I get to fuck some shit up?'

'Loads,' assured Grandma.

'Okay let's do it.'

Chapter 21

'How did we get this footage?' asked the accountant.

'Drone,' answered Colonel Hislop.

'I don't remember authorizing that expense.'

'Look, Godfrey,' snapped the Colonel. 'I authorize expenses, you are a simple bean counter. Understand?'

The accountant nodded, a scared little gray man in a world of warriors. But still, he was unhappy. He was meant to authorize any expense over six hundred dollars, and it was obvious from the quality of the images they were watching that the equipment providing it came to a damn sight more than that.

There were six other men in the room. All contractors.

They were all that was left of Colonel Hislop's core local team.

Together they watched the attempted hit unfold, from the first shots on the freeway, to the destruction of the sign, and finally, to the end of the team.

'Holy shit,' stated one of the contactors. 'We're gonna need a bigger boat.'

'Really? Outdated movie jokes at a time like this?'

'Come on, colonel, Jaws was a classic.'

'Did you see the same thing I saw?' questioned the accountant, with more than a little disbelief in his voice. 'Fifteen men died. And that thing? That wolf person thing? You people are unfeeling monsters.'

'Hey, Godfrey,' said the Colonel. 'It is what it is. Clearly, this is a huge setback. To lose men like that is very upsetting to us all. But war is war, sometimes shit happens. Now, Parker,' Hislop addressed the man who had made the boat quip. 'Any suggestions?'

'There are a few people I can think of,' responded Parker.

'No,' gasped Godfrey. 'We need to stop. This is untenable. Whatever the hell that thing was out there, what if it comes for us?'

'That's why we got to bulk up our personnel,' said Parker. 'Get more guns onboard. Come on, lighten up, after all, there's enough money for everyone.'

Godfrey tilted his head to one side at the mention of money. 'How much exactly?'

'One hundred million dollars, as long as we get the job done,' said Hislop.

Godfrey sat still for a while as his accountant's brain did the math. After a few seconds he nodded. 'What about that South African outfit?' he offered; all fear crushed by avarice. 'I heard they were looking for work. Also, the new company operating out of the Bahamas, Primary Defense, something like that.'

Hislop smiled. 'Welcome to the party, Godfrey. Right, people, let's put together a force that will be capable of taking that nightmare down. Spare no expense.'

Godfrey was about to object to Hislop's last comment, but then he decided it wasn't the right time. After all, a reward of one hundred million did allow for quite a large leeway when it came to expenditure.

And for the first time in his life, Godfrey actually thought – hell yeah, damn the expense.

Chapter 22

Suki arrived just over twenty minutes after the others.

Now they stood together in one of the lounges.

Griff and Brenner were smoking, while Solomon poured whiskies for them. He didn't ask anyone's preference; they all got a generous slug of Laphroiag single malt Scotch. No water. No ice.

If you didn't like it – tough.

Standing next to Suki was the man she had brought from the penthouse.

'This is Sergeant Maximillian Keller. He is a Knight of the Holy See, sent by the pope to help us. Well, to help Brenner specifically.'

Solomon handed the Knight a glass of Scotch. 'A Knight of the Holy See, that's impressive, I heard you chaps can kick some serious ass. So how do we address you? Sir Max?'

Maximillian shook his head. 'Officially, I am addressed as Grandmaster Keller, but Max is fine by me.'

'Good, well then, Max,' continued Solomon. 'Talk to us.'

Before Max could begin, the air in front of him shimmered, then with a crackle of power and the stink of ozone, a portal opened and Grandma stepped through, surrounded by her ethereal light.

Max took one look and dropped to his knees.

'Angelica,' he said, his voice throbbing with reverence.

Grandma smiled at him and laid her hand on his head. 'Stand, Grandmaster,' she greeted. 'Call me Grandma.'

'You know he's a Knight?' asked Solomon.

'Of course,' answered the Malak. Then she walked over to Griff and kissed him hello.

'Okay, Max,' continued Grandma. 'As Solomon said, talk to us.'

Max bowed again, then he took a sip of his whisky to calm himself before he began.

'His Holiness sent me to assist mister Brenner,' he started.

'Just, Brenner, kid,' said Ded. 'No mister.'

'Okay,' acknowledged Max. 'Papa informed me that Brenner was an Authority of heaven. He also told me that his partner was pregnant with the Messenger. As is laid out in the Great Plan.'

'Hold on,' interjected Brenner. 'Firstly, how does he know all this, and secondly, Messenger?'

Max frowned. 'He knows because the Pope is infallible,' answered Max. 'And the Messenger is the forthcoming voice of the people. The conduit between all of humanity. A sort of universal translator and communicator.'

'I don't get it,' said Brenner.

'Your child is the bringer of peace,' explained Grandma. 'Well, strictly speaking, one of the possible peace bringers. The Messenger will be able to transcend politics, race, religion. Everything. They will allow humanity to discuss world problems without being influenced by power or greed. In other words, the ultimate facilitator.'

'Okay, fine. Still not sure if I get it.'

'The child is very important,' continued Grandma.

'Yeah,' said Brenner. 'I know that. And I didn't need no Knight to tell me that. So, do you know where Shadow is?'

Max shook his head. 'Sorry, sadly I do not. But the church has bent all of its power to finding out. And as soon as they know anything, Cardinal Sandri will contact me.

'The cardinal also told me to inform you that you are being hunted by many different factions. Demon spawn, para-military groups, government agencies, and soon, even members of the general public will join in. There is currently a huge bounty on your head.'

'Tell us something we don't know,' quipped Griff. 'We've already run into a couple of them.' He turned to Grandma. 'So, my angel,' he said. 'What you been up to?'

Grandma told them. Not about her visit to the Watchers, but about creating a raft of Brenner simulacrums and sending them out on the road to confuse the enemy.

Griff chuckled. 'Hold on,' he said. 'So instead of one huge, ugly, cantankerous mother, we now got… how many?'

'The witches got one,' answered Grandma. 'Then I laid one over Rufus 'Fucking' Johnston, another on the polar bear, Logan Logan. Another on Saul, the werebison, and the last on Conrad, the grizzly. Then I sent each of them off with at least ten other clan members. Whoever runs into one of the fake Brenner's is going to be in a world of hurt. Those shifters are truly going to fuck shit up.'

Max looked shocked at the angel's cussing.

Griff laughed at the Knight's expression. 'Yeah,' he quipped. 'And she smokes and drinks and gambles.'

'This all helps,' said Brenner. 'And thank you. But it's not finding Shadow.'

Grandma nodded. 'Look, I also spoke to those insufferable Watchers. Asked them to help.' She shrugged. 'I wouldn't hold my breath though, sticklers for the rules those two, although I don't blame them, they are literally in charge of time and fate. But don't fret, big man. Everyone is looking for her.'

'Cool,' said Griff. 'So we gotta get out there as well and make some waves. First things first. You got weapons, transport?' he asked Solomon. 'I need to do a stock take and prep us so we ready to rock and roll ASAP.'

Solomon nodded. 'Sure. Follow me.'

They all followed the man in black, along a corridor, through another reception room and then down two flights of stairs into a deep basement.

He walked up to a large steel door and tapped in a code on an adjacent keypad.

The door swung open to reveal a vast armory, complete with a selection of vehicles.

And in prize of place, in the middle of the room, stood a Winnebago Horizon.

Griff stopped dead and stared, his face a picture of lust.

'Dude,' he croaked. 'Awesome.'

'Over forty foot of highly customized luxury,' said Solomon. 'Only one bed. For emergency use, didn't design it as a camper. Raised suspension, Kevlar armor. Run flat tires, bullet resistant glass. An electronics suite that looks like something out of NASA.'

'Shotgun,' shouted Griff. 'That's mine.'

'You can't just shotgun a multi-million-dollar motorhome,' said Solomon. 'It's mine,'

'No way,' insisted Griff. 'It *was* yours. Everybody knows I'm the Winnebago dude.'

Suki laughed. 'Fine, Griff,' she said. 'It's yours.'

Solomon shook his head.

'Sweet,' said Griff. 'Now why don't you dudes all piss off while uncle Griff sorts the kit out.'

The rest of the team, barring Grandma, left the room, heading for something to eat.

Chapter 23

The Watchers.

Dressed in their ethereal garb.

White robes that shimmered with light. White boots of finest kidskin. Strapped to their waists, rapier-like swords sheathed in diamond and pearl encrusted scabbards.

But the biggest difference to their usual appearance was the wings. Folded on their backs. They spanned thirty feet if extended, and were covered in the finest silver-white down.

The only recognizable thing about them were their pale blue eyes – and the clear, ever-full bottle of shine the one carried

Michael stared at them, his arms folded, as they lounged in a pair of wingback chairs, drinking shine.

'You have broken the rules,' he stated with a sneer.

'Uh-uh,' denied mister Reeve. 'Haven't.'

'At very least, you are interfering,' insisted the Archangel. 'And that in itself could influence the Great Plan.'

'No,' replied mister Bolin. 'We watch. That is all.'

'But you are considering doing more,' accused Michael.

Both of the Watchers shrugged.

'How would you know?' asked mister Reeve. 'Now bug off Michael. You sanctimonious pain in the butt.'

'You forget yourself, Reeve.'

'That's mister Reeve to you. And fuck you very much, mister Archangel. We bin doing this gig for millennia and you dare to question us now?'

'I grow wary of your attitudes. As such, I have asked for permission to call upon one of the Seraphim to discipline you both.'

The Watchers stood, power coruscated about them and they visibly grew in stature.

'You go too far, Archangel,' said mister Bolin. 'Your time as a warrior has eaten away what little sense you ever had. You forget, you are a mere soldier. We are time itself. If we do not observe, it cannot come to pass. Without us, there is no here, no now and therefore no past. We are one with the universe. We are one with the power. We are the universe and it is us.'

'You assume to command us,' added mister Reeve. 'But how can one command time? How can one ordain what has not yet happened? We do what we have to do, Michael. But your pride has driven you to take this personally.'

Lightening crashed about the two old men, and storm clouds filled the air. They spread their wings and the light of heaven bathed them in holy fire.

'It is you who forget yourself, Michael,' continued mister Reeve.

Michael took a step backwards as the combined power of the Watchers almost overwhelmed him.

And he remembered. The beginning. The end. The Alpha and the Omega.

None could exist without the Watchers.

They were the firmament that held all together.

But he had forgotten. Over the millennia he had come to see them as what they portrayed.

A pair of meddling old men.

As opposed to the very engineers of the universe.

The craftsmen who laid the very building blocks of time itself.

He closed his eyes as their light became too bright to behold.

And when he opened them, they are gone.

But they had left their bottle of shine

The Archangel fell to his knees and wept.

They had left their ambrosia.

And without it, soon they would no longer be immortal. They would become human.

And all time could end.

'Oh, dear Lord,' cried Michael. 'What have I done? Forgive me my hubris.'

And all around the world, the darkness pressed a little closer.

Chapter 24

Hopkins worked in the basement of the black-ops building, like a troglodyte. He rarely saw the sun. Or other human beings.

As a result, his social skills were minimal.

But his technical skills were second to none.

To the point where little challenged him anymore. It was difficult to get Hopkins excited with any task.

Until now.

The boss had put him in charge of locating Brenner. And until recently, it had proven impossible. It was as if the man had simply ceased to exist.

But now he had something to tell the boss.

He knocked hard on Miller's door and barged in, waving a piece of paper in front of him like a flyswatter.

'What the hell, Hopkins,' yelled Miller. 'You can't just crash into my office like that.'

'I knocked, sir.'

'Yeah, but you didn't wait for an answer. That's what knocking is for. You rap politely on the door, then you pause.'

'Yes, knock, pause. Got it.'

'Okay, what you have there?'

Hopkins waved the paper even more wildly. 'I got him,' he said. 'That Brenner suspect.'

'Hold on,' said Miller as he hit the intercom button on his desk. 'Johnson, Carlton, get in here.'

Seconds later the two men in suits raced in to the office.

'Hey,' noted Hopkins. 'They didn't knock.'

'Sut up, Hopkins,' said Miller. 'Now, tell us where Brenner is.'

'You just told me to shut up,' whined Hopkins. 'Must I talk or be quiet?'

'You know, Hopkins,' sighed Miller. 'If you weren't a goddamn genius I'd have shit-canned you years ago. Just tell us.'

'He's near the Canadian border. Wisconsin. A little no horse town, Broken Stump Junction.'

'Yeah, we got him,' yelled Johnson as he turned to high-five Carlton.

'Hoorah,' shouted Carlton. 'Don't mess with the American government. We got the tools and we got the … whatever.'

'Right, Johnson,' said Miller. 'I want you on point with this one. Carlton, two IC. Get together a double combat team. Twenty men. I want the best we got. And I want you boys in Wisconsin yesterday. By that, I mean I want you outta here in the hour. Move it.'

***

'I feel the same as I always did,' said Greta quietly as she looked down at Brenner's simulacrum that surrounded her body. 'It's just super weird.'

She sat in the dark corner of a biker bar on the outskirts of a small town that went by the moniker of, Broken Stump Junction. With her were ten more Kriegshexen.

When they had first entered the bar two days prior, some of the bikers had made a few sexist comments.

Penelope, one of the smaller members of the combat team, had taken three of them outside and beaten the ever-loving shit out of them.

No one commented any more.

Then they had recognized Brenner. Or at least, who they thought to be Brenner.

'Hey,' said Carlos, the head of the local biker gang, Coyote MC. 'It's the dark rider.'

'No way,' yelled other members as they crowded around, eager to see the man who was a living legend amongst the biker community.

The witches kept them back. 'Please, guys,' urged Penelope. 'The big man wants a bit of alone time. I'm sure you understand.'

'Sure thing, missy,' answered Carlos. 'And if there's anything we can do, you just tell us.'

'Actually,' responded Penelope. 'There is.'

So, for the last two days, the entire gang were acting as lookouts along every possible entrance and approach to Broken Stump Junction.

One of the members walked into the bar and approached, pausing until Penelope beckoned him forward.

'Samuel, is it?'

'Yes, ma'am,' responded the biker with a grin.

'Wassup?'

'They're here,' he said. 'Some sons of bitches just flew in on a couple of science fiction airplane helicopter hybrids. About two dozen of them. Looks like they're coming straight here.'

Penelope smiled. 'Well, let's get ready then.'

Chapter 25

The enemy team landed about two miles outside of the town. Far enough away not to alert anyone to their presence due to the V-22 Osprey chopper planes.

Then they proceeded on foot towards their destination.

Greta sent two of the witches to keep an eye on the advancing team, and they kept in contact via good old fashioned cell phones. No magical telepathy, no encrypted radios. Just phone calls and texted images.

The enemy team had done their research, they knew the layout of the town, the approximate population and the general surroundings.

They were well trained and handpicked for exactly this type of work. Armed with a selection of assault rifles, light machines guns and hand grenades. Dressed in the latest black Kevlar combat gear, and sporting high-end comms and helmets.

They were ready for anything.

Or so they thought.

But what Greta and her *Kriegshexen* had done was a stroke of tactical genius. Using a full coven and calling on the power of the surrounding land, the witches had created a huge illusion. It wasn't perfect in every detail; in fact, some parts were mere suggestion as opposed to identical reproduction.

But it would be good enough to fool most anyone.

So, when the combat team approached the town of Broken Stump, they had no idea that they were still half a mile from their destination, and what they were looking at was actually the *Kriegshexen's* illusion of the self-same town.

The difference being, what they were actually walking into, was a perfectly formed natural ambush siting, enhanced by the narrow valley that led into the town.

As they entered the kill zone, Greta had her witches flood the area with fireballs.

Then they followed up with short accurate bursts from their submachine guns.

At the same time, Greta banished the illusion.

It was perhaps the sudden disappearance of the town that caused the attackers the most consternation.

'Holy shit,' yelled Johnson. 'Where'd the fucking town go?'

'Incoming,' shouted Carlton.

'I know there's incoming,' screamed Johnson. 'The place is full of incoming. What I want to know is where are we? Have we just been teleported? Where are the buildings? Who is shooting at us? What the fuck is going…'

Johnson's tirade was brought to an abrupt end as a sizzling fireball blew his head off.

It was a testimony to the training and disposition of the government team that most of the men were firing back, albeit in long, panicked bursts. But they were still fighting, even though, to all intents and purposes, they had gone from a town, to a valley full of fire and lead and death.

Carlton began to rally his men. 'To me,' he shouted. 'Return fire, keep low.'

And slowly, a semblance of order was brought to bear as the black-ops agents started to look for targets as opposed to firing indiscriminately.

So, Greta decided to up the ante.

Six of the witches activated a pre-prepared spell. A powerful wind commandment. Swirling, drawing, pushing until a small whirlwind started to form. Then, as they fed more and more power to it, it grew into a raging tornado.

Then the next six witches added fire.

'Stick this for a ball of wax,' yelled Carlton as he saw the spinning raging firestorm bearing down on him. 'Run. Back to the choppers. Move.'

As one, the team sprang to their feet, turned and ran.

But you cannot outrun the wind.

Less than a minute later, the fire-tornado struck the two V-22 Osprey's.

Not one of the black-ops team survived.

***

Miller and the team of five comms experts stared at the huge, hi-def screen that showed them a real-time satellite image of what was happening outside of Broken Stump.

And, quite frankly, it was almost unbelievable.

'What the crap' yelled Miller. 'Where is that ordnance coming from? Where is the artillery?'

'No artillery in sight, sir,' responded one of the comms technicians.

'Bullshit, then what the hell is dropping those bombs on my team?'

'Sorry, sir. Can't say. We're expanding the search.'

'Holy crap,' screamed Miller. 'What is that?'

The formation of the tornado and the subsequent firestorm left the entire room speechless as they watched the team get wiped out, and then could do nothing to stop the fire-tornado from engulfing the Ospreys and destroying them.

The entire battle lasted less than two minutes. Miller didn't even have enough time to get on the radio and talk to any of them, or warn the Osprey pilots.

The operation was an unmitigated disaster.

As he stood staring at the burning airplanes, another comms person rushed into the room.

'Urgent message, sir,' he announced.

Miller turned to him, his face still slack with disbelief at what he had just witnessed. 'What is it?'

'He's been spotted, sir.'

'What? Who? Where?' stuttered Miller.

'Brenner. He's in Texas. Border of Mexico. Place called Hangman's Gulch.'

'That's impossible,' denied Miller.

'No sir,' insisted the specialist. 'We have eyes on.'

Miller sat down with a sigh. 'What the actual hell is going on?' he groaned.

Chapter 26

In most corporations, the higher a person was in the pecking order, the higher their office was in the building.

To be summoned to the top floor was to be called before the king. Or whatever the corporate or government version of royalty is.

In the murky world of government black ops and under-the-table dealings, quite the opposite is usually in effect.

In other words, the more powerful the person, the deeper they were.

For example, the Pentagon has an official two-story basement.

In reality, it is rumored to go more than twenty floors down.

And to descend to those rarified levels is akin to descending into hell.

Charles Miller was currently ensconced in a small high-speed elevator, plunging downwards into those very halls of darkness.

He was not confident that he would make the return trip.

After all, his last operation had been less than stellar. Actually, it had been a complete fuckup. He had lost both teams, plus almost two hundred million dollars' worth of equipment. It was just as well he wasn't in the game for the reward, as he was already so deep in the red, he was drowning.

And to make matters even worse, Millers communications and tracking experts were now getting eyes on Brenner all over the country - at the same time.

What a goddamn awful cockup.

No siree, Millar was under no illusion he was being called to the depths for a pat on the back.

The elevator hissed to a halt and the door opened to reveal two uniformed, armed men. Miller felt their close resemblance to the black uniforms of Hitler's SS was not a mere coincidence.

They beckoned for him to follow.

No one spoke.

The corridor stretched out in front of Miller, a seemingly endless walk to the gallows. Finally, they arrived and the Nazi lookalikes opened a door, ushered him in and closed it behind him.

Miller wasn't sure what to expect. Men in dark cloaks, maybe subdued lighting, shadowy corners and a general feeling of menace.

Instead, it looked like the boardroom of any successful Fortune 500 company.

Six slightly overweight men in hand tailored suits sat at the table.

A wet bar in the corner, jugs of water on the table.

Along the one wall, a huge television screen showing a live feed of the city outside.

Miller felt a wave of relief wash over him. This was not a room where people went to die. At worst, this was a room where one got a severe telling off, and perhaps a sideways promotion to the arctic circle.

Then one of the men looked up and Miller caught his eyes.

Absolutely soulless. It was like the abyss staring back at you.

And once again, Miller was afraid.

Deathly afraid.

'Sit down,' said the soulless man.

Miller obeyed.

As one, all six men turned towards him. He felt like someone had thrown a bucket of icy water over him, such were the feelings of dread that pervaded his mind.

A desperate need to apologize for his failings almost overwhelmed him, but at the same time, his mouth was so dry he simply could not speak. Instead, he managed a tiny croak, then stopped trying.

'You have let us down,' said the first man.

Miller did not reply. After all, it wasn't a question.

'It falls on us to decide what to do with you now.'

Still, Miller did not react.

'I tell you what, Charles,' continued the man. 'Why don't you make a suggestion.'

Miller cleared his throat. Then he leaned forward, grabbed the water jug, filled a glass and then promptly knocked it over.

A small part of him noticed that the water flowed away from the men, as if they repelled it.

It drained into his lap, leaving him looking like a toddler who had just wet his pants.

'Sorry,' he mumbled as his brain tried frantically to come up with some sort of worthy response.

None of the men commented.

'I can do better,' he managed, his voice hoarse with fear. 'I swear.'

'We are sure that you can,' said the first man. 'After all, Charles, you can hardly do worse.'

'I do not think you appreciate the importance of this mission,' interjected one of the other men.

Miller noticed for the first time that if he actually looked, all of them seemed almost identical. The same height, same weight, similar suits, watery blue eyes, fleshy jowls and over generous, wet, cherry red lips.

There were subtle differences, but they were more like Cabbage Patch dolls than human beings.

'Yes,' affirmed another. 'You must realize, exterminating Brenner and his cadre is this nation's highest priority.'

'The highest,' stressed another Cabbage Patch doll.

Miller noted their voices too were as close as dammit to identical.

'I can do it,' urged Miller. 'I will need some more resources, but I guarantee success.'

None of the men spoke for a few minutes. The silence stretched out like a desert.

Miller began to sweat.

Finally, the first man spoke. 'You shall get everything you need. We will spare no expense. Personnel, weapons, transport. Satellites, drones, every and anything you need. But if you fail us again, Charles …'

He left the sentence unfinished. There was no need to state the obvious.

One of the men flicked a card across the table.

Miller picked it up. Metal. A lustrous golden color. His name, Charles Miller engraved on the one side.

On the other side, the words, O *potens obscurum, per quem omnia incenduntur.*

Miller's Latin wasn't even high school level. He assumed it was some stupid government motto.

If he had even a basic knowledge, he would have known it read – O Mighty Dark Lord, by whom all things are set afire.

'This is your soul-linked card,' explained the first man. 'It is your passport to power.' He opened his briefcase, removed a small leather-bound notepad and passed it to Miller. 'Here is a list of all the people you can call on. Show them the soul-card and they will acquiesce to both your smallest and largest needs and wants.

Miller flicked through the first couple of pages and was stunned at the names. Generals, politicians, famous Hollywood actors, well known charismatic church leaders and high-up government officials.

'Really?' he asked. 'These people will listen to me? Follow my orders?'

'If you show them the soul-card.' The first man slid another piece of paper across. 'Sign this,' he instructed.

Miller didn't dare ask what it was, he simply took out his pen and signed. As he did so, he felt a wave of darkness rush through him. But just as quickly as it had occurred, it was gone.

'And finally,' continued the man, as the door opened and a woman walked in and stood next to Miller. 'Miss Johansen will need a couple of samples. Place your hand on the table.'

Miller frowned, unsure as to what was actually going on.

'Do it,' snapped the man.

So, Miller did. Hesitantly placing his hand on the table.

He flinched as miss Johansen placed her one hand over his, and then, she deftly clipped three of his fingernails and placed the nail clippings in a small glass jar.

Then she took out a pair of scissors and took a small sample of his hair that she placed in a second glass jar.

After that, she left the room.

Miller stood stock still for a while, waiting for his next instruction, totally baffled as to what had just transpired.

'All done,' informed the man. 'You can fuck off now.'

Miller put both card and book into his inside jacket pocket.

As he did, the door opened and the two guards reappeared.

'I won't let you down,' he said with as much conviction as he could muster.

Then he held his hand out to the first man.

The man looked at him as if he had just offered him a slice of fresh dog shit.

Miller blushed in embarrassment, turned and left.

Half an hour later, he was in his car, heading back to his offices.

Chapter 27

Michael stepped forward.

He had been summoned.

And although he held his head high, and ensured his wings stood out slightly from his body to enhance his overall aspect, he was ashamed.

The original and the most serious of the seven deadly sins.

The belief that one is essentially and necessarily better, superior, or more important than others. Failing to acknowledge the accomplishments of others.

He had forgotten his own lack of divinity, and he refused to acknowledge his own limits, faults, or wrongs.

He was an Archangel.

But he was not divine.

And now he stood before the six-winged. The Seraphim. Headed by Seraphiel himself, the leader of the eight judging angels.

'Kneel, brother,' said Seraphiel. Then he turned to Jehoel. 'Our brother comes before us to be judged. Will you speak for him?'

Jehoel said naught. For he was the Angel of Silence, and Seraphiel's request was mere custom. There was no defense when you were called. If you were not guilty, you would not be at the judging.

'Brother,' continued Seraphiel. 'Would you speak on your own behalf?'

Michael shook his head. 'I supplicate myself before you as a sinner,' he said. 'Hubris has entered my soul. I was tasked with overseeing the Great Plan, and instead, I allowed myself to believe I was in charge of it, even questioning the knowledge and forbearance of the Watchers themselves.

'I crossed the thin line between righteousness, and self-righteousness.

'I offer myself up to be broken on the wheel. Let me re-learn humility, I beg of you.'

Time stretched out into infinity as the Seraphim judged.

And, yea did Seraphiel speak. 'You show contrition, brother,' he declared. 'And your desire for humiliation is virtuous. But we warn you, you overstepped, the Great Plan cannot be lorded over, or used for personal gain. It is, it always was, and it always shall be. You may go now, brother. Continue your good work and remember your place.'

Michael stood up, but he did not leave.

'Is there something else?' asked Seraphiel.

The Archangel took the half full bottle of shine from his pack.

'What is this?' whispered Seraphiel.

'They left it.'

The heavenly lights flickered, waxing and waning. The flames that made up Seraphiel's wings roared high, and the sound of war drums filled the air.

'Find them, Archangel,' commanded Seraphiel. 'Find the Watchers and give them back their ambrosia, before it is too late.'

Michael bowed once and left in a flash of holy light.

Chapter 28

The demon lord, Zobrondo, took a drag on his massive cigar, blew some smoke rings towards the ceiling and sighed.

He was seated in what was ostensibly a gentleman's club. Leather wingback chairs, deep burgundy carpeting, wooden paneled walls.

The only major difference to a normal version of such a club, were the rows of cages containing wailing, partly dismembered, naked human subjects. The stench of brimstone. And of course, the myriad of minor demons scurrying about the place, serving drinks, and various other sundry offerings and demands to the lords of hell.

'Why so glum?' asked the demon sitting opposite Zobrondo, another hellish noble called, Asadak.

'My latest assignment,' answered the demon lord.

He proceeded to tell Asadak about the Quartet warriors, and how easily Brenner and his companions had destroyed the European team.

Asadak nodded. 'All humans are idiots,' he declared.

'I agree,' answered Zobrondo. 'But these are allegedly well-trained deadly warriors, and the wolfman treated them like they were nothing. Less than nothing. I fear that even if I send the entire crew, all three teams, they shall fare little better.'

'You're missing the point, Zobrondo old man,' countered Asadak. 'You need to get a lot more demonic on the whole problem. Stop messing around with these mere mortals the Quartet have given you. Use them as bait, or just kill them yourself for fun. Whatever, you need to up the ante. I myself am a huge fan of possession. Get some of your lowly minions to possess a bunch of humans, and use them to attack this Brenner chap. And go large, good fellow. I'm talking thousands here. That should shake things up.'

Zobrondo didn't answer straight away as he contemplated the advice. To be honest, possession wasn't his strong suite. He could do it, of course, but ostensibly, he was more of a battle demon.

And even if possession was his bag, with the Archangel Michael and the pair of insufferable Elohim, the so-called Watchers, being in charge of preventing things like mass-possession, there was little chance he would succeed. They were simply too powerful to fight against.

And there was no chance of them being taken out of the picture.

However, he had to admit to himself, Asadak was correct, he had been going about it the wrong way.

'How would you like to get in on this?' he asked the demon lord. 'Could be good for your rep. And between the two of us, we could raise a veritable army of possessed.'

Asadak didn't respond.

'It involves the Great Plan,' urged Zobrondo, keen to get Asadak involved. 'We would be sticking it to them big time.'

Asadak smiled. 'Why didn't you lead with that?' he asked. 'Yes, old chap, I'm in. Now, when and where shall we start?'

Zobrondo grinned. With help, maybe he still stood a chance. Now if he could just convince a few more demon lords to join him, he could take the fight to Michael and the Watchers.

Chapter 29

The bar was called, Baron Samedi.

Named after the Haitian loa of the dead.

And it was situated in a part of New Orleans that literally angels feared to tread.

Most angels, that is.

Two old men walked inside.

Both were dark skinned with long gray hair and blue eyes. Bushy gray beards, semi formal clothing. Open necked white shirts, dark suits, patent leather shoes. The clothes were neat and clean and so threadbare that you could almost pick out the individual strands of the weave.

The one went and sat down at a table in the corner, the other walked on up to the bar.

'You got shine?' he asked.

The barman, who was busy polishing a glass with an obligatory greasy cloth, sneered at the old timer.

'Fuck off, hillbilly,' he grunted. 'This ain't no Appalachian, mountain shack.'

'What you got that's good?'

The barman shrugged. 'Got some Gentleman Jack.'

The old man slid some notes across the counter. 'Bottle,' he said. 'Two shot glasses.'

The barman grabbed the cash, did a quick count, noted it was more than triple the amount needed, and pocketed it before fetching the bottle and glasses.

Mister Reeve carried them back to the table and sat down.

'What's that?' asked mister Bolin.

'The barman's best. Apparently.'

He poured a shot for each of them

They threw them back together, and both grimaced.

'It's been a while,' noted mister Reeve. 'But was human alcohol always this bad?'

'I reckon so,' answered mister Bolin. 'Still, no doubt it shall do the trick.'

'I suppose,' granted mister Reeve. 'But it ain't no ambrosia.'

'He poured two more shots.

Within minutes the level of the bottle dropped below half.

Ten more minutes and mister Reeve stood up. 'Better get another bottle,' he said. 'I don't remember it being this weak.'

He walked up to the bar once more and called the barman over. 'Another bottle of your whisky,' he said, again sliding far too much money across the countertop.

The barman raised an eyebrow, but he wasn't going to say no to the veritable cash cow that had just wandered into his establishment.

However, mister Reeve's casual overpayment had not gone unnoticed by many of the other patrons of the establishment.

Very unsavory patrons.

Mister Reeve sat down and poured. But before he could take a drink, a group of three men pulled up chairs and sat down at the table without asking.

'Hey, old man,' said one of them, obviously the ringleader. 'How abouts you buys us all a drink?'

Mister Reeve didn't even bother to look up. 'Not that kinda angel,' he said. 'You'se must have got us confused with the Cherubim.'

'Yeah,' interjected mister Bolin. 'We don't do charity. Ain't our gig. You need be looking for Rikbiel, or Sachiel.'

'Maybe even one of the Virtues,' added mister Reeve. 'Israfil, perhaps Eleleth.'

'No, he's a Luminary,' corrected mister Bolin.

'Oh, yeah. Not him,' admitted mister Reeve.

The newcomer stared at the two old men. 'Just what you talking about?' he snapped. 'Actually, doesn't matter. I see you got a lotta cash, now I reckon, if you wanna leave this bar in one piece, you better hand it over.'

Mister Reeve sighed. 'Go away.'

The man pulled out a switchblade and flicked it open.

'You wanna rephrase that?' he growled.

Mister Reeve backhanded the thug so hard he drove him out of his chair and flung him across the room, smashing him into the far wall.

His unconscious body slumped limply to the floor.

The other two newcomers stood, drawing blades as they did.

Mister Bolin frowned, then he too stood up.

And his wings sprouted from his back, almost filling the room, such was their span.

'Sit down,' he thundered. 'Everyone, sit. Do not move. My friend and I are having a quiet drink, when we are finished you can move again.'

Every person in the room was as still as a statue.

Even if they had wanted to move, they were unable to.

A Watcher had commanded them, and as such, it was humanly impossible to disobey.

But you could still see their emotions in their eyes.

Some were terrified.

Some ecstatic.

Some overwhelmed.

For they had seen a holy power, and it was magnificent.

Mister Bolin sat down. 'You know something, mister Reeve,' he said, as he poured another shot. 'I am sure that the world has a much higher preponderance of assholes than it used to.'

Mister Reeve took a sip before he reacted. 'Perhaps,' he ventured. 'But if I recollect, the time around the Salem Witch Trials, the world went pretty long on assholes then. And the Spanish Inquisition were not the nicest of people.'

'Yeah,' concurred mister Bolin. 'And that's just amongst our lot.'

'Maybe we've just become less forgiving of late,' suggested mister Reeve.

'Perhaps. But it still feels that the world has gotten rather bullish when it comes to creating dickheads.'

'I do second that motion,' said mister Reeve.

'Tell you what,' continued mister Bolin. 'Why don't we drink a few more bottles of this barely acceptable alcohol and then just see where the evening takes us.'

'A splendid suggestion, mister Bolin. Why don't we?'

Chapter 30

'Why did we come to New York?' asked Jethro. 'The place smells real bad and it's full of strange people.'

'I always wanted to visit the Big fucking Banana,' replied Rufus in his Brenner simulacrum.

'Apple,' corrected Jethro. 'Big Apple.'

'Whatever,' snapped Rufus. 'Some fucking fruit.'

The group of mountain lion shifters stood on the sidewalk outside Grand Central Station.

Rufus 'Fucking' Johnstone, Jethro, Otis, Harlan and Evelyn. They had been chosen by virtue of the fact; they were the best combatants in the clan.

'Where to first?' asked Evelyn.

'Rueben's Deli,' said Rufus. 'Heard they serve pastrami sandwiches as big as a cow's head.'

'How do we get there?' asked Otis. 'Catch a cab?'

'Fuck that,' replied Rufus. 'We fucking walk.'

'We don't know where it is,' pointed out Evelyn.

'It's famous,' said Rufus. 'We'll just fucking ask some local.'

That said, the Brenner lookalike turned to a pair of male pedestrians walking by. 'Excuse me, sirs,' he said. 'I wonder if you could…'

But before he could finish, the men, who were totally ignoring him, simply walked on by.

Undeterred, Rufus/Brenner turned to a single female.

With an almost identical result.

And then a trio of teenagers.

'What the fuck?' yelled Rufus. 'Am I like fucking invisible? Did this Brenner thing turn me into the invisible fucking man? Evelyn, you try, I think there's some weird shit going on here.'

Evelyn had marginally more success, as one couple did vaguely acknowledge her presence, in that they shook their heads and gave her an emphatic, 'No.'

'I think they're all just dicks,' suggested Otis.

'Well fuck that. I'm Rufus Johnstone, and I don't take this shit from no fucking city slickers.'

'Umm, boss,' interjected Otis.

'What?'

'Actually, you're Brenner.'

'Oh, fuck, yeah. Well then, I'm Ded Brenner, and now I most definitely don't take no shit from these peons. I'm a godsdamn living fucking legend.'

With that, Brenner/Rufus walked over to a group of three besuited men who were discussing something that involved a lot of back slapping and raucous joviality.

'Excuse me,' said Rufus. 'Do any of you gentleman happen to…'

Almost as one, they turned to him and shook their heads. One managed a quick, curt, 'No.'

Rufus stepped forward, moving in between the trio of men, getting real close. Then he delivered a short, sharp jab to two of the men's temples, knocking them instantly unconscious.

Before either of them could fall to the sidewalk, Otis and Evelyn stepped forward and held them up, arms thrown companionably around their shoulders, their shifter-strength making it look totally natural.

Rufus got right-up in the last man's face. 'Now listen to me, you slick faced, sorry fucking asshole, I'm gonna ask you a fucking question, and then you are gonna fucking answer it. You fucking get me?'

The man nodded, face pale, fear sweat beading on his forehead.

'Rueben's Deli, heard of it?'

'Yes, sir.'

'Good, directions.'

The man pointed west. 'Keep down that way. Past Union Square. Then turn left into East First Street. You can't miss it.'

'There,' said Rufus. 'That weren't so fucking difficult, was it?'

The man nodded.

'Now, because you been so fucking helpful,' continued the lion-shifter. 'I ain't gonna kill you.'

The man closed his eye. 'Please,' he whispered.

'Remember, fucking manners maketh man. Now here.' Rufus grabbed the two unconscious men and propped them up against the third man. 'You hold your fucking friends up. We're off. Bye now, and you have a nice day.'

And the group of shifters dispersed, moving so fast as to look like they had simply teleported away from the scene.

Six minutes later, as opposed to the sixty minutes a normal person would have taken, they were standing outside the deli.

Rufus led the way inside and they sat down in one of the booths. The booth was for eight people, but the five shifters filled it to overflowing, their supreme grace belying their actual physical bulk.

A waiter walked over and started to hand out some menus.

'No need, guy,' said Rufus. 'Just tell us what the biggest fucking sandwich is.'

'That would be the Rueben's, mile-high pastrami on rye.'

'Cool, give us ten of those and a bunch of sodas.'

'Sir, the sandwiches are rather large. Most people can't even get half way through. Unless you're planning to take a few home.'

'Ten fucking mile-highs and soda,' repeated Rufus.

The waiter raised an eyebrow and left.

In quick time, the waiter returned with an assistant. Each carried a tray of five sandwiches with side helpings of pickles and cans of soda.

And while they obviously weren't a mile-high, they were respectably humungous.

With a smirk the waiters deposited the food on the table.

'Just give me a shout when you want me to get you a takeaway box,' the main one said as he left.

Mere minutes later, the waiter responded to a holler from Rufus.

'Could we get the fucking check?'

The waiter did a classic double take, then he bent over and peered under the table, finally he walked around the booth, staring closely at the occupants and the immediate surrounds.

'Okay,' he said. 'Where did you put the food.'

Otis rubbed his stomach. 'Inside us,' he answered. 'It was good. Nice snack.'

'Bullshit,' blurted the waiter. 'No one can eat that much in just a few minutes. 'Am I on candid camera? Is this some sort of joke?'

Rufus sighed. 'You know, we ain't been in the Big Fruit for but a few fucking hours, and I have come to the unescapable conclusion that everybody in this city is a rude fucking asshole.'

'Hey,' reacted the waiter. 'It's New York, man. What did you expect?'

He tore off a ticket and handed it to Rufus. 'Pay at the cashier. Service charge isn't included in the check.'

'Yeah,' acknowledged Rufus. Then he turned to Otis. 'What the fuck is a service charge?'

Otis shrugged. 'Might be he thinks we need our car serviced or something. Who knows, these city folk are right weird?'

'Fucking idiots,' mumbled Rufus as he got up to pay. 'Right, where to next?'

The team spent the rest of the day doing every tourist thing they could think of. Including the Empire States building, the Statue of Liberty and the 9/11 Memorial.

Night time found them completely lost in Brooklyn, wandering a few miles from Times Square as they went looking for a hotel.

Five country bumpkins.

In Brooklyn.

Lost.

It was time for the night-feeders to come out.

Because to the average gang-banger, this group looked ripe for the plucking.

And unbeknown to the shifters, they had just walked past the main hangout of the Brooklyn Crips.

'Hey, Efrem, what those redneck honkies doing in our hood?'

Efrem took a drag of his cigarette and looked out of the window of the brownstone that acted as the gang headquarters and residences. In fact, they controlled the entire row. Four buildings, all of which should have been condemned many years before.

He stared at the group, and then took a step back. 'Shee, mu-fuka,' he exclaimed. 'You know who that is?'

Kordell shrugged. 'Some bunch white mo-fo's.'

'No way, my man,' contradicted Efram. 'That's the mutha with the bounty on him. You know, the gazillion dollar one.'

'For real?'

'For real, man,' concurred Efram. 'Get the rest of the boys. Whoever in the house. Tell them to tool up, move.'

Kordell ran to obey.

A couple of minutes later, there were seven of them. More were coming, but Kordell reckoned seven was enough to wrap things up. After all, this was gonna be like shooting fish in a bucket.

All the Crips were armed with the same weapons, they had just taken supply of a complete shipment of them.

The Skorpion submachinegun, chambered for the .32 ACP round. A small, not hugely effective round for general combat, but for drive-by shootings and close work, it was more than adequate.

Combined with its insane rate of fire, over nine hundred rounds a minute, and a twenty-round magazine, this cheap

Czechoslovakian machine pistol is perfect for untrained thugs and gang-bangers.

However, there are two major problems with the package, firstly, at that rate of fire, the entire twenty round magazine is expended in just over one second.

And, secondly, due to its short barrel and awful balance, the Skorpion is wildly inaccurate at any distance over a few feet.

Of course, there was a third major problem. But that didn't even enter the heads of any of the street thugs that were lining up at the window, ready to hose the small group of strangers with lead.

And that third problem was – if you shoot a shifter with a .32 ACP round, all you are going to do is piss him off.

'Ready?' asked Efram.

There was a general mumble of agreement.

'Right,' he pushed the window open. 'Kill those mothers.'

The crips opened fire, expending one hundred and forty rounds of ammunition in just over a single second.

Some of the rounds struck their target.

Most didn't.

'Yeah, they going down,' shouted Efram. 'We just got Snoop Dog rich.'

'Uh, Efram,' squeaked Kordell.

'You what?'

'What the hell is that?'

Efram looked at their intended victims. But something was wrong with whole picture.

None of them had actually gone down. Also, it was as if his eyes were fooling him, because he no longer saw a group of five redneck honkies.

Instead, he saw…

'Fuuuuuuck,' he warbled, fear driving his voice into the high upper registers.

The things in front of him were no longer human. They were huge and hairy and full of muscles and teeth and claws.

And they were running towards them at a speed that belied belief.

Before any of the gang bangers could react, the were-lions crashed through the window and tore into them.

Rufus/Brenner had morphed into his human/lion mode, while the rest of the pride had gone full were-lion.

Inside of six seconds, all the gang members were dead. Save the single one that Rufus had kept aside for questioning.

The sounds of the shooting, and Kordell's earlier warnings, had alerted the rest of the gang, and the sounds of running feet were approaching.

'Otis, Evelyn,' commanded Rufus. 'Door. Kill them all.'

The two lions smashed through the door, not even bothering to open it.

Then sounds of more gunfire, screams of terror and loud roaring filled the night.

Meanwhile, Rufus had Efram off the ground, holding him up by the front of his shirt.

'Okay, sonny, fucking talk to me, why you all shoot at us?'

'What…what are you?' stammered Efram.

'I'm Rufus 'Fucking' Johnstone,' replied Rufus.

'Uh, boss,' interjected Jethro, who had assumed his hybrid mode in order to talk.

'Oh, yeah. Forget. I mean, I'm Ded 'Fucking' Brenner.'

'No, what *are* you?' repeated Efram.

'Oh that, I'm a fucking werewolf.'

Efram looked puzzled. 'You look more like a mountain lion.'

'Don't let the lion thing fool you,' said Rufus. 'That's the other me, but when I'm Brenner I'm a wolf. Just not really, on account of me being a lion. Get it?'

Efram shook his head.

'Doesn't matter. Why you shoot at us?'

'There's a price on your head,' answered Efram. 'Like a hundred million dollars.'

'Who told you?'

'Not sure, everybody knows. It's like the word on the street. They even got photos of you and shit.'

Before Rufus could respond, Otis and Evelyn walked back in, still in lion mode.

'All done?' asked Rufus.

Otis growled softly and nodded in response.

'Cool, we gonna need some clothes for when we change back,' stated Rufus. 'I reckon we take a look around the place.'

'What about him?' asked Jethro, gesturing towards Efram.

'Oh, fuck him,' said Rufus as he threw the gang banger against the wall so hard, he actually left an imprint in the plaster, before he sank to the floor, every bone in his body shattered beyond repair.

Ten minutes later, the shifters were back in human mode and dressed in the latest crip street fashion.

'Hey, all these dudes' clothes is fucking blue,' noted Rufus. 'I mean, like all of it.'

'Yeah, I think it got something to do with gang colors or some shit,' said Otis.

'Like a fucking school uniform?' asked Rufus, genuinely interested.

'I dunno,' admitted Otis. 'Nice shoes though,' he commented on the British Knight sneakers he was wearing.

'Hey, check this out,' said Harlan as he entered the room. 'I'm Mister T.'

He had around thirty pounds of gold chains and medallions around his neck.

'That's ridiculous,' said Evelyn. 'And who's Mister T?'

'Really?' scoffed Harlan. 'The A Team? I pity the fool? B. A. Baracus?'

'Yeah, just saying random words is not going to make me know who he is, but whatever, you wanna look like some sort Bling Ho, you go for it.'

'How many of these fuckers did you and Otis off?' asked Rufus.

'Not sure,' answered Evelyn. 'Maybe thirty or so. Didn't count.'

'Reckon there's more of them?'

'Like, in the city, or here?'

Rufus shrugged. 'I mean, in the city. Close by. Because Brenner's got a massive price on his head, and it looks like every gangster in New York is gonna be gunning for him. I was just thinking, maybe we do a bit of pre-emptive striking. Thin out the uglies in this neighborhood.'

'Shouldn't be that difficult to track some more down,' conceded Evelyn. 'And I suppose we would be doing the public some good.'

'Yeah,' agreed Rufus. 'So, we're all in? Let's go kill some fucking gang bangers.'

'Yeah, I pity the fools,' interjected Harlan.

'Hey, Harlan,' said Rufus.

'Yeah.'

'Fucking shut up.'

Chapter 31

Suki ran into the room. 'We've got incoming,' she informed everyone.

'Incoming?' asked Max, the Knight of the Holy See.

'An enemy attack,' expanded Suki. 'The radar tells us at least five airborne. Helicopters, judging by their speed.'

'Griff, is everything ready to bug out?' asked Brenner.

'Of course,' confirmed the old man.

'Let's go,' said Solomon. 'My bet is, they are going to hit us hard. I have some serious counter-measures in place, but we want to be as far from here as possible, as quickly as possible.'

Solomon led the way as they all jogged to the armory.

'To the Mirth-Mobile,' yelled Griff as they entered.

'You named a million dollars of custom, high-tech Winnebago after that shitty car from Wayne's World?' scoffed Solomon.

'Hey, that was a 1976 AMC Pacer,' argued Griff. 'A classic.'

'I refuse to travel in a vehicle called the Mirth-Mobile,' said Solomon.

'Schwing,' replied Griff.

'Boys,' said Grandma. 'I have no idea what you're talking about, but could you please get your heads in the game?'

'Sorry,' mumbled Griff as he opened the door to the Winnebago and clambered into the driver's seat.

The rest of the team followed suit, Brenner riding shotgun and the others getting in behind him.

'What's their ETA?' asked Griff. 'Because if they're real close, they gonna blast us as soon as we exit.'

Solomon grinned. 'That will not be a problem,' he stated. 'We have an alternative exit. Griff, head towards the back of the armory.'

Griff raised an inquisitive eyebrow, but didn't say anything. He knew Solman well enough to know he wasn't a big fan of idle chatter. Starting the vehicle, he drove slowly across the vast armory.

When they were twenty feet from the rear wall, Solomon hit a remote on his cell, and with a low grinding sound, the wall slid to one side to reveal a badly lit, roughly constructed tunnel that stretched into the distance.

'This comes out almost a mile from the Ranch,' stated Suki. 'Drive carefully, it's a bit rough and ready, but it should be safe enough as long as you don't treat it like a race track.'

'Groovy,' said Griff as he eased the Winnebago into the tunnel, flicking the powerful headlights on to provide some much-needed illumination.

As they moved forward, the false wall slid closed behind them.

Meanwhile, Suki opened her laptop and brought up a live feed of the skies above the Ranch.

'What's that?' asked Max.

'An unpleasant surprise for the helicopters,' answered Suki. 'It's a remote launching system for three Starstreak missiles.'

'How did you manage to get to get hold of those?' asked Max. 'Isn't that strictly government issue only?'

'Sure is,' answered Suki as she used her mouse to operate the camera, scanning the skies as she spoke. 'Put it this way, these babies cost around a hundred K each, plus the launch system. We paid over three hundred K for each one. There's very little a huge pile of money can't sort out.'

Griff turned to try and look at Suki's screen.

'Hey,' warned Brenner. 'Eyes front, dude. Suki's got this, you just make sure we don't crash into the tunnel wall and get buried alive.'

That said, the rest of the team crowded around Suki, eyes glued to the scenario that was beginning to unfold on screen.

On the far horizon, five helicopters hove into view.

'Looks like…' Brenner paused. 'I have no idea what those three are.'

'Let me see, let me see,' yelled Griff as he tried to sneak another look while keeping his eyes forward.

Brenner lifted the laptop and showed the old man.

'Holy shit,' cussed Griff. 'Those don't officially exist yet. It's the prototype, Sikorsky X Raider. Heavy firepower, fast, stealth capabilities. Dudes, this is some serious high-end government equipment. We ain't dealing with contractors or US Army here. These guys are off the charts.'

'The other two helicopters look like some variant of the Blackhawk,' added Solomon. 'Ten, maybe a dozen troops in each. Man, these guys are coming in hot and heavy.'

'Tracking the lead X Raider,' said Suki, as she manipulated her mouse. Then she hit enter. 'Starstreak one away.'

'You'll be lucky to hit those SOB's,' said Griff. 'They got mad skills.'

They watched as the hypersonic missile accelerated towards the target. The X Raider, cut hard right. At the same time a cloud of anti-missile flares exploded from the sides of the helicopter.

'That won't do you any good,' scoffed Suki. 'This baby's laser guided and has three beam riding submunitions.'

'As long as your aim is good to go,' interjected Griff.

No one spoke as they watched the vapor-trail head towards the helicopter, jinking to follow the pilot's maneuvers. Then there was a secondary flash as the main missile launched its three, tungsten darts.

Less than a second later, the X Raider exploded.

'Strike one, fancy new helicopter,' said Brenner.

Suki moved fast, tracking the next helicopter and firing.

This time, though, the X Raider climbed fast and then dropped, leaving the Starstreak to fly harmlessly past and self-destruct as it reached its ceiling.

The third missile flew true, and the second X Raider crashed into the ground before exploding in a pillar of fire.

By now the surviving X Raider and the two Blackhawks were in range, and all three opened fire on the ranch building.

The Blackhawks discharged their 70mm Hydra rockets pods in an orgy of destructive power, two hundred and eighty high explosive rockets bore down on the building, backed up by a stream of gatling gun fire.

At the same time, the X Raider launched a slew of Hellfire missiles.

Suki's camera tracked them coming, and then her screen went blank.

'Well, that's all she wrote,' quipped Brenner. 'Still, took out two of the asswipes.'

'That is just the beginning,' said Solomon. 'I would bet they are going to land and put troops on the ground, check the area out. And that's when my final shots will be fired.'

'You set the place to blow?' asked Grandma.

Solomon nodded. 'Like the fourth of July.'

'You are an evil man,' she chuckled.

Five minutes later, unseen by the team who were at that moment exiting Solomon's underground escape route, the helicopters landed and twenty-four troops debussed.

Solomon's fourth of July booby trap was not high on sophistication. It didn't involve lasers, or movement sensors or even pressure sensitive plates.

What it did involve were a bunch of old-fashioned trip wires surrounding the area, and around a ton of C4.

The resultant explosion was heard in Las Vegas.

The three helicopters, and the personnel were all but vaporized.

A little over two thousand miles away, in an underground bunker, the recently soul-carded Charles Miller stared at the satellite feed in open-mouthed amazement.

Four hundred million dollars of equipment and almost thirty men – gone.

And he still wasn't sure if he had terminated the target.

Although he sincerely doubted anyone could have survived that fiery holocaust.

Before he could contemplate his next move, a communications officer ran into the room.

'Sir,' he yelled. 'We got him. Brenner's in New York. Him and his crew just offed a bunch of gang bangers.'

Miller took a deep breath.

Then he opened his jacket, drew his Glock pistol, and fired the entire fifteen round magazine into the satellite viewing screen.

Chapter 32

'You reckon you got them all?' asked Brenner.

Solomon nodded. 'You heard the explosion.'

'Schwing,' quipped Griff.

'Okay, enough with the Wayne's World shit,' said Brenner. 'What brought that all on?'

'Streamed it last night,' answered Griff. 'Classic.'

'Well that strike confirms what we all knew. The government are coming for us.'

'Coming for you,' corrected Solomon.

'Whatever,' interjected Griff. 'The thing is, we need to hide. Get deep undercover.'

'Can't do that,' argued Brenner. 'If we're deep undercover, we can't look for Shadow.'

'Dude, we can't look for her at any rate, we don't know where to start,' said Griff.

'There must be something we can do. Grandma, help me,' urged Brenner.

'It's beyond my powers,' said Grandma. 'The Watchers might be able to cast some light on things, but,' she shook her head.

'Those boys haven't put a foot wrong since the beginning. I mean, sure, they push the boundaries, but they would never actually get involved. And in all fairness to them, who knows what might happen if they did. They Watch, if they acted on what they saw - fate, destiny, providence, perhaps even time itself could be affected.'

'What about me?' asked Brenner. 'I'm an Authority, don't I got no powers?'

'Loads, my sweet boy,' answered Grandma. 'Just not those sorts.'

'What powers do I have, then?'

Griff sniggered. 'Fucking shit up. That's your superpower.'

Before Brenner could argue the point, Griff's cell rang. He checked the number and passed it straight over to Grandma.

She took it, had a brief conversation and chuckled as she rang off.

'Looks like Greta and Rufus are creating the expected mayhem. And it does confirm what you just said, everyone in the entire world is gunning for you, big man.'

'What about the other shifters?' enquired Brenner.

Grandma shook her head. 'Nothing, not yet. But they aren't as forthright as Rufus or the witches.'

'We need a plan,' said Brenner. 'And I have no idea where to start.'

'Church,' stated Grandma.

'What?'

'We need to find a church,' the Malak continued. 'It's a conduit, big man. We need to speak to someone from upper management. See if we can get some sort of help.'

'Really, a church?' scoffed Brenner.

'Yes, moron,' snapped Grandma. 'That's what they're for. And you see, the Pope…'

May he live forever,' interjected Max.

'Yeah, what he said,' continued Grandma. 'Anyway, the Pope has sent us a Knight of the Holy See. And what most people don't know, those of the order of the Holy Sepulcher, or Holy See, are amongst the few mortals who can provide a direct conduit to the heavenly realms.

'Max is like our own private cell phone to the celestial sphere.'

'But what about you?' asked Brenner. 'And me, aren't we actual angels? Don't we get no preferential treatment?'

'We aren't those sorts of angels, Ded,' answered Grandma. 'Trust me, Max is out man when it comes to this. Now, Griff, look it up on your satnav thingy and get us there.'

'Your wish is my command, oh angelic one,' answered Griff.

'Asshole,' laughed Grandma.

Chapter 33

Logan Logan made an even better Brenner than the big man himself. Because although the magical simulacrum was really close, Logan Logan was so big they had to name him twice.

Almost seven feet and over three hundred pounds before he went full polar bear.

He and five other polar bear shifters had decided to go to the obscure town of Salmon Point on the western shores of Alaska. They made this decision for one main reason, Salmon Point, although isolated, had an excellent communications network, due to the fact that two major government research stations were situated close by.

And Logan Logan reckoned that if Grandma wanted the Brenner simulacrum to be tracked down, Salmon Point was a good place to go, as any reports could easily be broadcast. Also, it was small enough to get noticed in, and isolated enough to make any escape easy.

However, what Logan Logan did not know was, due to its location, geographical situation and the general corruption of its law enforcement, Salmon Point was a major transfer point for hard drugs into the state.

Particularly those smuggled in by Dominican drug lords.

As it was winter, the polar bears had gone for snowmobiles as opposed to Harleys. Logan Logan's one was a black rat-bike version, in keeping with Brenner's legend.

There was only one hotel in the town, the Grand Central. It was neither grand, nor was it central, being situated on the outskirts of the town.

But it was relatively clean, and most importantly, had vacancies.

After checking in, the team of shifters walked to a nearby dive bar. Hugo's. A buzzing neon sign outside boasted of Cold Beers and BBQ.

Pickups, motorbikes and snowmobiles filled the snow-covered parking area. The sounds of a live band drifted past the closed doors.

Country music. Loads of banjo and fiddle.

Not bad.

The shifters pushed the doors open and walked in.

Needless to say, they attracted attention

Four men and two women. All six foot plus. Even the girls weighed in at just under two hundred pounds. No fat.

Logan Logan went up to the bar.

'Beer. Anything domestic.'

'Got Corona on special offer,' advised the barman.

'Gimme a dozen.'

The barman grabbed a metal bucket, loaded the beers into it and threw a few handfuls of ice on top.

He handed it to Logan Logan who paid in cash. 'Keep the change.'

He walked over to the table the team had sat down at and placed the bucket in the center.

'That's a good idea,' commented Sheila. 'Beer in a bucket. I like it.' She helped herself to a bottle, chugging it down in one long swallow.

'What now, boss?' asked Peter.

Logan Logan shrugged. 'Not sure. I suppose we just hang about until something happens.'

'What if nothing happens?' continued Peter.

'Grandma told me that something would happen. She reckons Brenner has this, I dunno, like power. Whenever he gets involved with something, shit just happens. I think she called him a Discordian or summat.'

'Need more beer,' interjected Sheila.

'Get it yourself,' said Logan Logan.

'Sure,' responded Sheila. 'I'll check what food they got as well.'

As Sheila stood up, the doors opened and a crowd of men poured in. They were all of a type. Swarthy, patent leather dress shoes, shiny suits, chunky gold wristwatches, large rings on all fingers, roughly shaven with hair slicked back.

If there had been a neon sign above them flashing the word, trouble, their obvious criminal demeanors couldn't be more noticeable.

The general hubbub in the bar ceased and Logan Logan noticed two of the patrons exiting, leaving their drinks unfinished.

The group walked up to the bar.

'I thought you were arriving tomorrow,' stated the barman.

'Came early,' responded one of the men. 'Rum, a few bottles.' He turned to stare at Sheila. 'You're a big one,' he sneered. 'Come, sit with us.'

Sheila chuckled. 'I think not.'

'It wasn't a request,' snapped the man. 'So, take you pretty ass over to that table and wait for me.'

This caused Sheila to burst out laughing. 'In your dreams, little man,' she scoffed as she walked back to the table.

'Trouble?' asked Logan Logan when she sat down.

Sheila shrugged. 'Possibly.'

'Inbound,' murmured Peter. 'Looks like they're packing heat.'

'I'll pack their heat,' rumbled Logan Logan.

'That makes no sense,' noted Sheila.

'I know,' admitted Logan Logan. 'Sounded better in my head.'

The man who had commanded Sheila join him, stopped at the table, flanked by his cronies. 'Listen I'm going to forgive you, just this once,' he said. 'Because you're new here, and you obviously have no idea who I am.'

'Oh, but I don't want to be forgiven,' purred Sheila. 'I've been a bad girl, and I should be punished.'

The other shifters did a not so good job at concealing their laughter.

'Stop it,' said Logan Logan. 'You're not so funny. Just tell him to piss off so we can go back to drinking in peace.'

'Hell, a girl can't have any fun with you,' quipped Sheila. 'Okay,' she continued as she addressed the thug. 'What's your name?'

He raised an eyebrow, his brain not having quite caught up to the unexpected turn his threats had taken.

'I am Julio.'

'Cool. Fuck off, Julio,' said Sheila. 'There's a good boy.'

'How dare you?' hissed Julio.

'Logan Logan noticed the other patrons in the bar, including the barman, were taking cover. Ducking behind tables, the bar, some even piling out of the windows.

'Gun,' yelled Peter.

Logan Logan moved fast, placing himself between Julio and Sheila.

The report of the pistol was deafeningly loud in the enclosed space as the thug drew, pointed and pulled the trigger.

Twice.

A neat double tap that spoke of both familiarity and training.

Both nine-millimeter rounds struck Logan Logan in his upper chest.

They would have hit Sheila on the face.

The room went silent as everyone waited for the big man to fall to the ground.

Logan Logan flinched slightly as the lead rounds struck home, and then he spoke.

'Hey, you dick,' he growled. 'You shot me. That's not nice.'

And in one smooth movement he picked up his chair and smashed it over Julio's head, driving him to the floor and fracturing his skull.

The rest of the thugs went for their guns.

'Control,' bellowed Logan Logan. 'Don't change.'

But he was too late. Already, Sheila had burst into her polar bear form, shredding her clothing as she went from a mere six foot, two-hundred-pound human to a nine hundred pound, ten feet tall beclawed, monster polar bear.

The thugs opened fire at her, but they may have well been pissing on a forest fire for all the difference it made.

Sheila-bear threw her head back and roared. The windows rattled at the sheer volume, and bottles of liquor fell from the shelves as the entire building shivered as if in an earthquake.

The rest of the shifters stood back. Sheila was on the rampage, and a mere dozen armed thugs were not going to be able to stop her. There was no need for them to get involved.

A few minutes, about fifty rounds of ammunition, and a bunch of broken bones and squished internal organs later, it was all over.

The various patrons came out from behind the tables, and the barman popped up from behind the bar.

Sheila was still in full polar bear mode, standing in the corner, not even breathing heavily as her advanced healing pushed the few slugs out and healed her wounds.

'How did that bear get in here?' asked the barman.

'It changed,' said one of the customers. 'Just before the shooting started, that girl changed into the bear.'

Logan Logan grabbed his rucksack and pulled out an oversized shirt. Then he walked over to Sheila bear who morphed back into her human form and quickly donned the shirt. It was large enough to reach down to her knees like a dress.

'Thanks, chief,' she said. 'Sorry about that. When the shooting started, I lost it.'

'Can't be helped,' said Logan Logan as he turned to the barman. 'Who are these dudes?' he asked, gesturing at the fallen thugs.

'Dominican drug dealers,' answered the barman. 'They come in her once a month. Usually on the last Wednesday of each month. They're early.'

'So, if it's a regular thing, how come the cops don't do nothing about them?'

The barman shrugged. 'They're all on the take. Corrupt pieces of shit. Look, mister,' he continued. 'I don't know who, or what you guys are, but we want no part of it.'

'Tough,' said Logan Logan. 'You are a part of it now.'

'We won't tell anyone,' stressed the barman.

Logan Logan chuckled. 'Don't really care,' he said. 'Ain't no one going to believe you if you do.'

'True,' admitted the barman. 'A word of warning then, there are more of them. Normally about twenty of them come in. They arrive at the docks with their own ship, full of drugs. Look, I gotta call the cops. Even if they are corrupt, we can't keep the fact that there's a bunch of dead guys in the bar.'

'They ain't all dead,' argued Sheila.

'Pretty much,' said the barman, and a few of the customers mumbled their agreement.

Peter and the rest of the shifters did a quick check.

'Wow,' said Peter. 'Girl, you did a real number on these guys.'

'Hey, they were shooting at us. Fair game, self-defense. Anyway, pieces of shit drug dealers. Live by the sword and all that.'

'Come on,' said Logan Logan. 'I reckon we need to blow this joint, maybe pay a visit to the ship the barman was talking about. Preemptive strike.'

'Might as well,' agreed Peter. 'It's what Brenner would do.'

The shifters trooped out, leaving a group of stunned and shocked locals who's lives would never be quite the same again.

***

'It's not as big as I thought it would be,' said Sheila. 'When he said ship, I was expecting something huge.'

'Yeah,' agreed Logan Logan. 'That's more superyacht than ship. Still big though.'

'Armed guards,' noted Peter. 'One on the gangway, at least two more on the deck.'

'How we going to do this?' asked Sarah, the other female shifter.

Logan Logan shrugged. 'I'm not really a strategist. Any ideas?'

'What would Brenner do?' asked Sheila.

'Probably just walk on board, kill everyone, and sink the boat.'

'Works for me,' said Peter. 'Hell, those guards are rocking hand guns, we go bear or hybrid mode and just fuck shit up.'

Logan Logan nodded. 'Peter, you and me go hybrid, the rest, full bear, you're less likely to get hurt that way. But we'll need at least a couple of us to open hatches and shit.'

The shifters disrobed and loaded their clothes into the rucksacks they had brought with them. Then, as one, they changed.

Eschewing any form of stealth, Logan Logan decided to opt for full shock-and-awe instead.

And it worked.

Initially.

The armed guard on the gangplank didn't even begin to react as the five shifters charged towards him, three in full bear mode, and two in their hybrid half-human, half werebear form.

He saw them coming, but his brain was so flooded with what seemed like impossible stimuli, he simply stared open mouthed until Logan Logan dispatched him with a single swipe of a massive paw.

The two guards on the deck reacted a little better, one drawing his pistol and firing, while the other pulled out a whistle and blew a series of sharp blasts.

Neither reaction did them any good as the bears leaped onto them and literally ripped both of them in half.

Logan Logan led the charge into the interior of the boat, yanking doors off and smashing the surrounding superstructure to enable the massive werebears access.

More shots rang out as the bears proceeded into the various staterooms and cabins, wreaking inordinate amounts of havoc as they smashed their way through all obstacles.

Logan Logan entered one of the master suites to find two women cowering on the bed, scantily clad and over made up.

'Get out,' he growled at them.

They didn't move, terror rooting them to the spot.

'I said go,' commanded Logan Logan, gesturing at the smashed open doorway.

This time, the two girls bolted, grabbing their coats as they did.

The sound of automatic gunfire rent the night, and Logan Logan turned and sprinted. Sidearms weren't a big problem, but even werebears couldn't easily shrug off an assault rifle.

Dashing back onto the deck, Logan Logan saw Peter was down, bleeding from a multitude of hits. Glancing up, the bear alpha saw a man standing on the top of the wheelhouse, in his hands an AKM assault rifle.

Instead of charging him, as was his usual wont, Logan Logan looked around for a weapon, finally grabbing a cork lifebuoy ring, emblazoned with the boats name.

San Cristobel.

It didn't weigh much, probably around six pounds.

Logan Logan threw it like a discus. It struck the gunman in the chest and the sounds of his ribs breaking was clearly audible, even over his screams of shock as he was catapulted over the side of the boat, into the freezing waters of the harbor.

The alpha ran over to Peter. 'Go full bear, man,' he yelled. 'Concentrate.'

Peter grimaced as he willed his body to morph from his hybrid form into full polar bear mode. Because they all knew the bear was the most resilient body shape they could have. Tougher, stronger and many times more aggressive, it would give Peter the best chance of surviving his wounds.

At the same time, the rest of the shifters gathered around.

Sheila morphed back into her human form, ignoring the subzero temperatures like it was a balmy summer day.

'Boat's clear,' she said. 'Found a few wooden crates full of what seems to be cocaine in the hold. Plus, two suitcases of pills. Don't know what they are.'

'Smash them all open and chuck them overboard,' instructed Logan Logan. 'Anyone got an idea on how to sink this tub?'

The rest of the shifters changed back to human form, all completely comfortable with their nakedness, and like Sheila, oblivious to the cold.

The only one who hadn't changed was Peter, who was sticking to his werebear form as he continued recovering.

'No idea, boss,' ventured one of the shifters. 'Sea cocks? Bilge pumps? Who knows.'

'Tell you what,' said Logan Logan. 'Let's just go down to the engine room, see if there's any gas or diesel or something, find some flares and just set the darn thing on fire.'

Half an hour later, the shifters were back on their snowmobiles, heading home. Behind them, the superyacht blazed high, like a celebratory bonfire.

Around ten minutes after that, someone strode into Charles Miller's office.

'He's in Alaska,' they informed him. 'Multiple witnesses. He's just taken out a drug ring and sunk a ship.'

Miller stared at the comms expert and then shook his head. 'Just fuck off,' he grunted as he sank further down into his chair, at a complete loss as to what to do next.

Chapter 34

Shadow had lost track of time. The dungeon was barely lit by a couple of smoky, flickering torches. And sometimes they went out, leaving her in almost pitch-black darkness.

Not that it inconvenienced her that much. Her night vison was superlative.

Her jailers were all demons. Not large, around four feet tall, small leathery black wings like oversized bats, deep red skin, yellow eyes, hairless. They wore filthy loincloths and stank of rotting meat and brimstone.

Every now and then they would slide a bowl of gruel and a jug of water into her room. Opening a small hatch in the bars to do so.

Although she was still chained, she was no longer held against the wall. Now her chains allowed her to walk the length and breadth of the cell, from her sleeping area, a thin straw mattress, to the odiferous waste hole in the corner.

She had no idea why, but she was still unable to access any of her shifting ability. Obviously, the demon lord who had imprisoned her was simply too powerful, and was somehow blocking her true soul.

However, she mediated constantly, searching for any hint of her inner self. Delving deep into her subconscious.

And in the last few days, she had begun to feel a tiny glimmer of her power.

The lion was there, but still tantalizingly out of reach.

Once again, she assumed the lotus position, calmed her mind, and journeyed deeper and deeper into herself.

There was no way she was going to let these shit-for-brains defeat her and steal her child.

No.

Way.

Chapter 35

'There's a church,' said Brenner.

'That's a BBQ shack,' argued Griff.

'Next to it, you ass.'

'Oh, sorry. My bad.'

Griff pulled the Winnebago into the churchyard and cut the engine.

The team disembarked, Grandma leading the way. Solomon waited until the rest had entered the church, then he made a lightning-fast dash for the building, limiting his exposure to the sun to less than a second.

He still came out in a rash of facial blisters, but they healed up fast, visibly changing from raw flesh to clear skin in a matter of seconds.

The church was small, maybe fit for sixty people at most. Wooden chairs as opposed to pews, a single stained-glass window, faded paint, well worn, but scrubbed clean as an operating theater.

They heard a door open at the back entrance and someone entered.

An ancient lady hobbled in and squinted at them, blinking while her eyes adjusted from the bright sunlight outside.

Brenner was about to speak, but she held up her hand to stop him.

'I can see this is way above my paygrade,' she said. 'I's gonna call the pastor, he in the BBQ shop. Wait.'

'Ma'am…' began Brenner.

What, you deaf or summat?' she snapped. 'I said to wait.'

With that, she shuffled back out, humming softly to herself as she did.

A few minutes later, she returned, accompanied by a large man in denims and an apron that read, *Soul food*, on it.

'You the pastor or the chef?' asked Brenner.

'Both, my son. We sell BBQ for the Lord. Help to keep the church funded.'

'See,' stated the old lady. 'I tell you they was a special case.'

The pastor nodded. 'You speak the truth, Elouise.' The pastor studied each one of them, nodded slightly when he contemplated Grandma, and Brenner and Griff. He smiled at Max, but when he looked at Suki, he looked puzzled. Finally, his gaze rested on Solomon, and he took a step back, crossing himself as he did so.

'Really?' said Solomon. 'You don't care about Brenner, but I get a double take and a warding? I'm just a common garden variety vampire, that SOB is the Prince of fucking Darkness.'

'Oh, Lordy, Lordy, Lordy,' mumbled the Pastor.

'He's fine, father Wilson,' said Grandma. 'He gives off an evil presence, but he's trying hard to be good.'

'You know my name,' stated the pastor.

'Of course she does, you dull witted nincompoop,' said the old lady. 'She be an angel.'

'I know,' answered father Wilson. 'I'm not blind. It's just, well, this is all a little overwhelming.'

'How can we be of service to ya'll?' asked Elouise.

'Wouldn't mind some BBQ,' ventured Griff.

Grandma gave him the eye.

'Maybe later,' he mumbled, looking at the floor and scuffing his feet.

'We just need a bit of alone time in the church, pastor,' continued Grandma.

'Can I stay?' asked father Wilson.

'How strong is your faith?' enquired Grandma.

Father Wilson looked slightly angry as he answered. 'I am a priest.'

'So?' scoffed Grandma. 'You wouldn't be the first holy man who's lost his way. The reason I ask is, I am not sure what will happen, but I can assure you this, whatever transpires might test your faith. So, if you are lacking, or questioning it, rather leave.'

Father Wilson nodded. 'I will stay.'

'Good man. And you, Elouise?'

'My faith is strong,' confirmed the old lady. 'But my heart, not so much.'

Grandma smiled. 'You need not worry about that. You might be tested, but I will not let you die of a heart attack.'

'Then I too shall stay.'

'Close the doors,' instructed Grandma.

Father Wilson obeyed, locking them as he did so.

'Right, how does this work?' asked Brenner.

'We need to build a bonfire in the exact center of the apse behind the altar,' answered Grandma. 'Then we strip naked and dance anticlockwise around it, shouting and rejoicing.'

'No way,' gasped Brenner incredulously.

'Of course not, you idiot,' snapped Grandma. 'We go to the altar with Max, and he kneels and prays. How else?'

Brenner had the grace to look suitably embarrassed. 'Sorry. Will it help if we all do it?'

Grandma shook her head. 'You, Max and me should do it. The rest of you, sit down and give us some positive thoughts.' She looked at Solomon for a few seconds. 'Especially you,' she added. 'The Lord forgives a lot. But you have most definitely pushed the boundaries.'

The man in black nodded. 'I'll do my best.'

'Is there anything specific we gotta say?' asked Brenner.

Grandma sighed. 'What don't you get about this, haven't you ever prayed before?'

Brenner shrugged. 'I was in 'Nam, any soldier who has been under fire has prayed.'

'There you go, Ded,' said Grandma. 'You don't even need to say it out loud, just relax and ask for help.'

'Got it.'

The three knelt before the alter and bowed their heads.

Max began to whisper something in Latin.

Brenner simply asked for help.

Grandma started talking. 'Hi,' she began. 'It's me, obviously. Look, we're in a bit of a bind here. Need some help. I know there's the whole Great Plan going on, but the thing is, I haven't really been involved with that. I do know I was responsible for protecting the big man and Shadow, so, in that task, I have failed.'

'It's not your fault,' interjected Brenner.

'Ded, shut up, I'm talking here,' snapped Grandma. 'As I was saying, forgive me, and please help us.'

Nothing happened.

'Well, what now?' asked Griff.

'Patience, my love,' scolded Grandma.

Seconds turned into minutes, and minutes into an hour.

The whole time, Max stayed at the altar, head bowed, hands clasped together. Praying silently.

And then the room exploded with light.

Blinding.

Like being enveloped in pure white fire.

But it didn't burn.

And then the sounds of an angelic choir.

A million, million voices singing at once.

Both uncomfortably discordant, and incredibly beautiful at the same time.

Then once again … nothing.

'Oh, come on,' said Griff. 'Now what? We wait some more?'

'Griff, enough,' said Grandma. 'This is important.'

'Yeah, sure,' scoffed the old man. 'Please hold. Your call is important to us. You are currently number four hundred gazzilion in the queue – your wait time is approximately – seven thousand years.'

As Griff finished complaining, there was a burst of light.

And standing in front of them, wings spread wide, surrounded by a halo of fire…

'Oh, shit, it's you,' stated Grandma.

The apparition bowed, 'Lamassu, I give greeting.'

'I no longer go by that name,' snapped Grandma.

'It is not your place to refute your calling,'

'Oh, fuck off, Michael.'

'This is Michael?' breathed Max in awe. 'The angel of mercy. The general of God's armies?' he fell forward, prostrating himself.

'He's also a gigantic pain in the ass,' scoffed Grandma. 'And sonny, that has got to stop, you can't just go around falling over every time you meet someone special. Get up. Now, what you doing here, Mickey?'

'I prefer, Michael.'

'And I prefer a less arrogant, stuck up…'

'Please, Lamassu, I am here to help. And also, to beg for your assistance.'

Grandma raised an eyebrow. 'I'm listening.'

Michael proceeded to tell them of his fall from grace. How he wanted to atone for his hubris. His arrogance. 'Until I feel I have atoned,' he finished. 'I am your humble servant. I will do as you wish.'

'Good,' said Brenner. 'Find Shadow.'

'How?'

'I don't know, you're the fucking angel.'

'So are you, what's that got to do with it?'

'This is the help we're getting?' said Brenner with a sneer. 'What's the point?'

'Hey,' argued Michael. 'I'm pretty good at fighting, you know. Heaven's premier warrior.'

'Yeah, well I'm not such a slouch when it come to that either,' informed Brenner.

'True. He's the king at fucking shit up,' laughed Griff.

Michael sighed. 'I will do all I can. I promise.'

Griff turned to Max, who had risen, but was still as pale as a shroud. 'Hey, boy, some serious shit going on here, you gonna be alight?'

Max nodded. But it was obvious he was in the process of experiencing a major existential crisis.

'Right,' said Brenner. 'Welcome to the team. Now let's try to get something done, I'm sick of just waiting for shit to happen.'

'Oh, and can we get some BBQ now?' asked Griff hopefully, turning to the pastor.

'Holy. Shit.' Cussed father Wilson.

Elouise punched him on the shoulder. 'Now don't you go cussing in front of the angels,' she scolded. 'Or I swear, I will beat the black off you. Now follow me, let's get ya'll fed.'

***

The team had eaten enough BBQ to feed a football squad, and they all agreed, it was fantastic.

Solomon had paid, and left a massive donation on top of the bill. Enough to fund the church for a year, at least.

Now they were all back in the Winnebago together.

Three angels, one of whom was also a werewolf, a Knight, a priestess of the Indian goddess Jyeshta, an old man who was now middle aged, and a vampire.

The beginning of the most complex *walks-into-a-bar* joke ever.

'I have something I need to say,' said Michael.

'Spit it out,' snapped Grandma. 'We're all friends here. Except for you, that is.'

Michael frowned but did not argue. 'I may have been a little economical with the truth,' he started.

'You mean, you lied,' clarified Brenner.

Michael shook his head. 'A lie of omission, perhaps. But I have told no actual untruth.'

'Michael,' warned Grandma. 'I said, talk.'

'I offended the Watchers.'

'I know,' acknowledged Brenner. 'You already told us. And to be fair, I can't blame you. Those two SOB's can be right ornery old assholes.'

Michael nodded. 'There is more.' He took a deep breath. 'Perhaps it is best I simply show you.'

And he pulled out a bottle from his pack.

Plain glass. Half empty – or perhaps half full, of a clear liquid.

He placed it on the table.

'Is that…' began Grandma.

'Hey, that's mister Reeve's moonshine,' said Brenner. 'Or is it mister Bolin's?'

Grandma shook her head, her features pale, her eyes slightly wild. 'Why?' she asked Michael.

'I insulted them. They informed me they had enough. Then they disappeared, leaving this behind.'

'Oh, Michael,' whispered Grandma. 'You arrogant fool, do you realize what you have done?'

The Archangel nodded, tears sliding slowly down his face.

'What's the big deal?' asked Griff. 'Some old dudes left their moonshine. So what?'

'Have you tasted it?' asked Grandma.

Griff nodded.

'Now think carefully before you answer, my love,' continued Grandma. 'What did you think of it?'

Griff gave the question the obvious respect Grandma had insisted on. 'It's most likely the best thing I ever tasted. No, it is the best thing I ever tasted, come to think of it.'

'That is because it is not shine,' said Grandma.

'It is Ambrosia,' explained Michael. 'The food of the gods.'

'And without it,' interjected Grandma. 'The Watchers will revert to being mere mortals.'

Brenner nodded. 'Okay,' he said. 'Not ideal, I admit. But so what? Two cantankerous old men will become mortal. No big deal.'

'They are the Watchers, Ded.' Said Grandma. 'If they do not observe, then it does not come to pass. They are the glue that holds the universe together. Second to the Almighty, they are the most powerful beings in the universe. And now they are simply two old men, alone, mortal and without purpose.'

'Without the Watchers,' continued Michael. 'There is nothing to stem the burgeoning of all evil. Even my great skills in battle are as naught if they are not there to behold it. They make reality. And without them, reality can become as warped and distorted as the darkness deems.'

No one spoke for a few seconds.

Then Griff said. 'Heavy.'

Finally, Grandma summed it up in a single sentence. 'We are so fucked.'

Chapter 36

The two old men walked out of the hotel reception, turned right and one minute later they were in the casino.

'Why do you want to do this, mister Reeve,' asked the one.

'Because, mister Bolin,' he answered. 'I would like to experience the randomness of humanity. If we ever gambled before, we would always win. Now, without our divine attributes, there is every chance we shall lose. I hope that might prove either invigorating, or at very least, informative.'

Mister Bolin nodded his acceptance of the reply.

Ten minutes later, the two of them were standing at the roulette table.

Mister Reeve purchased a small pile of hundred-dollar chips and placed one on the number twenty-two.

The croupier spun the wheel and called last bets.

The two old men watched the wheel go round and round, then the little silver ball bounced between the numbers and finally stopped.

'Number twenty-two, black,' informed the croupier as she stacked a pile of chips on top of mister Reeves bet.

Mister Reeve frowned. 'Can I just leave it there?' he asked.

The croupier nodded. It is still just under the house limit on numbers, sir. You may let it ride.'

'Let it stay then,' instructed mister Reeve.

Again, the wheel spun and the ball danced.

'Number twenty-two, black,' said the croupier.

There was a mummer amongst the other players, combined with a few envious looks.

Mister Reeve sighed.

'Could just be coincidence,' observed mister Bolin. 'You know, good old-fashioned chance.'

'Let it ride,' informed mister Reeve.

The croupier glanced over to the pit boss, looking for permission to accept what was now a bet of over one hundred and twenty thousand dollars. Another win would pay out in excess of four million dollars.

The pit boss talked into his chest mike, and then a few seconds later gave the croupier a nod.

The house had just informed him that the odds of the same number coming up three times in a row were over fifty thousand to one.

Everybody watched in silence as the ball tumbled and hopped.

'Number twenty-two, black,' said the croupier, her voice so quiet it was barely a whisper.

The people around the table went wild, clapping and whooping their congratulations.

Everybody likes to see the casino lose.

Mister Reeve took a deep breath, stood up and walked away from the table.

Mister Bolin followed.

'Sir,' shouted the croupier. 'Your chips.'

'Keep them,' said mister Reeve. 'After all, what's the point?'

Everyone watched the two old men leave.

The croupier shrugged, unsure what to do next.

Then the pit boss walked over and shut the table down.

'Strangest thing,' he informed the croupier. 'Heard this exact same thing just happened a few days ago in Vegas. Some lady won at poker, and then just walked away. Weird. Oh well, better get some higher ups down here to sort this mess out.'

And outside, mister Reeve tuned to mister Bolin, an expression of frustration on his weathered face. 'So,' he said. 'Still not human.'

'It appears that way,' confirmed mister Bolin.

'What now?'

Mister Bolin shrugged. 'Drink some more? Eat?'

'Might as well,' agreed mister Reeve. 'Can't think of much else to do.'

They continued down the street, looking for a likely restaurant.

Preferably somewhere that served seafood.

Chapter 37

Zobrondo looked upon the huge gaggle of cacodemons with absolute disdain. Strictly speaking, the small, twisted, deep red, humanoid monsters weren't even demons. They were, at best, mere malevolent spirits. They weren't even made of flesh. Their corporeal beings were some sort of phantasm. A type of physical apparition capable of transforming into spectral vapor with a thought.

This is what made them perfect for possessing a human host. Or any host, for that matter.

That was the only reason a lord like Zobrondo would even countenance being within spitting distance of the filthy little assholes.

'Looks to be about a thousand of the horrible shits,' assessed Asadak.

Zobrondo nodded. 'More than enough for a trial.'

'Brother, you seem hesitant.'

'I would be less worried if we didn't have to be with the cacodemons when this happens.'

Asadak laughed. 'Can you imagine?' he asked. 'Letting that herd of pig swill loose with no one to oversee them. They would start possessing cattle, family pets, cockroaches. Anything that was easier to control than a human being. No, we have to be there. And not only there, we have to be right amongst them to wield enough control to make this plan work. It will be fine, trust me, if anything happens, we'll be surrounded by a thousand expendables.'

'Trust you?' scoffed Zobrondo. 'A demon lord. Still, even with a thousand meat shields, if the Watchers appear, then next will be that asshat, Michael. Maybe even a few of his insufferable buddies. Not to mention, Brenner and his cohorts might even pitch up. Then what?'

'Then we run like buggery,' admitted Asadak. 'Hey, no pain, no gain. You ready?'

'Ready,' confirmed Zobrondo. 'Let's do this.'

***

Father Evans slapped his hand down on the table, but it did little to slow missus Jefferson's diatribe. The rest of the seven members of the town of Hartrock, Wyoming's annual town fair committee had long since given up trying to interrupt.

None of them, bar the father, were shy of seventy years old, and they knew from past experience, when Esme Jefferson started talking, all you could do was wait for her to finish.

So, they waited patiently, thankful for the air-conditioning in the church that at least allowed them to remain cool whilst suffering miss Jefferson's tirade.

'All I'm saying is,' she ranted. 'If we allow Pete Barton to judge the humorous vegetable contest again, he'll choose something that looks like someone's private parts. He always does. And I don't know about you, but I am sick of seeing vegetables shaped like tallywhackers or bongos.'

'Come on,' argued Tony Barker. 'They're vegetables, Esme, there ain't a hell of a lot of things a marrow or a cucumber can look like. And it's just a harmless bit of fun, we ain't talking some fancy art gallery or nothing.'

Before missus Jefferson could voice her displeasure regarding Tony's interruption, an inhuman scream rang out from close to the church boundaries.

The first one was followed immediately by a chorus of shrieks and doglike barking. But it was obviously not a canine.

'What in heaven's name?' questioned father Evans as he stood and walked over to the window.

'Who is it? What's happening?' demanded missus Jefferson, as she stood up and began to make her way to the window as well.

Father Evans held his hand up. 'Stop, Esme,' he said. 'You don't want to see this. Tony, you and Clive come here,' he continued, calling on the other two men in the room, and at the same time showing his innate concern for the women, as well as his inbred misogyny.

'I'll smack you upside your head, father,' snapped Esme. 'I'll be the judge of what I want to see.'

She bustled up to the window and peered out. The sounds of animalistic screeching and wailing continued unabated.

'Well, I'll be,' she said. 'Looks like the townsfolk have gone a little crazy.'

The rest of the members of the town fair organization committee flocked to the window and surveyed the scene unfolding outside.

The first thing they noticed was that Esme had a hereby unknown gift for understatement.

The townsfolk were not going a little crazy.

They were going absolutely, mind bending, shit for brains mental.

'Is that Pete Barton?' questioned Tony. 'What's he doing?'

'Looks to me like that vegetable pervert is trying to eat missy Petunia's face off,' stated Esme.

'Holy cow,' exclaimed father Evans.

The three other committee women, Lizzy Sharps, the town librarian, Dolly May and Eugenie Humphries, all sat glued to their chairs. Partly through fear, and partly because they were of the same misogynist bent as father Evans.

Clive stared out at the chaos. 'How come none of them is venturing inside the church grounds?' he asked.

Everyone turned to father Evans for an answer.

The father shrugged. 'Well how the heck should I know?'

'Because they ain't coming onto hallowed ground and you, being the preacher should know a bit about that,' snapped Esme. 'Tell you what, father, just give it your best shot. And do it quickly, there are folk dying out there.'

The father frowned, and thought for a few seconds before he spoke.

'As strange as this sounds, it looks like those poor people may have been possessed in some way. Not sure by what. But whatever it is, it must be pretty darned evil, because it fears the touch of hallowed ground.'

'Accepted,' confirmed Esme. 'So, what do we do to stop it? Them. Whatever.'

Father Evans hesitated. 'I…I…don't know.'

Esme reached out and grasped the young preacher by his shoulder. 'Brent Evans,' she said softly. 'I have known you since you were a little boy. You were never the fastest thinker, but you have always been solid. And you ain't no coward. So just collect your thoughts, and then tell us what to do.'

Father Evans nodded, set his shoulders back and went over his options.

'Holy water,' he suggested. 'And any blessed objects we have. They should help protect us. I think.'

'Holy water I know,' said Esme. 'But what are blessed objects?'

'Umm… I suppose they would be anything I bless.'

'Now we're getting somewhere,' said Esme as she delved into her voluminous handbag. Drawing out a snub-nosed Smith and Wesson 357 magnum. 'Could you bless Betsy?' she asked, waving the revolver around like it was a fan.

'Hey,' exclaimed father Evans. 'You sure you got the safety on that thing?'

Esme gave the preacher a look of absolute scorn. 'How can a man grow up in Wyoming and be so ignorant?' she scoffed. 'It's a revolver, you ninny. It ain't got no safety.'

'What if it goes off?'

'The revolver ain't possessed, father,' snapped Esme. 'Guns don't just go off. People just go off, like those poor possessed critters outside. Now, can you bless Betsy here?'

Father Evans frowned. 'Technically, I suppose so.'

'Technically? That means yes.'

Father Evans nodded.

'Well then say that,' snapped Esme. 'Anybody else tooled up?'

It was as close to a rhetorical question as possible without actually being one. As Wyoming has the highest number of guns per capita in America. Which might well mean, in the world.

Every person in the room, excluding father Evans, took out at least one firearm.

Clive drew two. One in a shoulder holster, and a small backup carry from an ankle holster.

Lizzy the librarian proceeded to take two matching Ruger SR40c pistols from her handbag. Then she placed four extra fifteen round magazines on the table. After that, she stood, and from a shoulder holster, and a pancake holster in the small of her back, she produced another pair of sub-compact Springfield XD's also chambered for the 40 S&W round.

Finally, from beneath the folds in her skirts, she took out a Ka Bar Bowie with a seven-inch blade.

Clive stared unabashedly at her. 'I think I'm in love,' he murmured.

'Why would you carry so many weapons?' asked father Evans.

'Why wouldn't you?' responded Lizzy.

'Okay, father,' interjected Esme. 'Get blessing. Then I'm sure Lizzy will loan you one of her weapons.'

'I won't carry a gun,' said father Evans. 'I'm not saying I won't fight, just not a gun. I will carry holy water, and that,' he pointed at the brass cross on the alter.'

'That's fine by me, Brent,' confirmed Esme as she held out her revolver.

The preacher took the weapon gingerly, then he knelt.

'Lord, at your word all things are made holy. Pour your blessing upon this…this…umm…'

'Smith and Wesson 357 revolver that goes by the name of Betsy,' interjected Esme.

'What she said,' continued father Evans. 'And grant that whoever makes use of it, will be doing so in your name.'

'Amen,' concluded Esme as she took her revolver back. 'Okay, the rest of you, line up.'

Two minutes later, father Evans concluded his last blessing. Then he collected as many bottles of holy water as he could from the font, picked up the heavy brass cross and stood next to Esme, a determined set to his face.

'Okay people,' ordered Esme. 'Let's get out there and do some good.'

Chapter 38

Lord Zobrondo was extremely impressive to behold.

Ten feet tall, built like Arnold Schwarzenegger circa mid-eighties, deep-scarlet hide, a classic forked beard, glowing red eyes, and a pair of large ram's horns that swept back on each side of his head.

And wings. Huge leathern, bat like wings that spanned a full twenty-two feet when unfurled.

Lord Asadak was no less impressive a specimen, albeit he was a full foot shorter. He was broader, larger horns, no beard and hide the color of blood from a freshly tapped artery.

And when the pair of them stepped out of the portal, into the middle of the Hartrock Main Street, the townsfolk's reaction was fairly predictable.

Especially when the two lords were followed closely by a swarm of stinking, ululating cacodemons.

Id Est – they went absolutely ape-shit.

To be fair, not everybody ran screaming. After all, this was Wyoming, so a bit of gunplay was to be expected, even from the most surprised of inhabitants.

But after three separate gunmen had opened fire on the lords to little effect as their rounds simply bounced off the iron-hard demon-hide, or just passed straight through the cacodemons without harming them, the general consensus seemed to become – *let's get the hell outa Dodge.*

But neither lord had time to revel in their spectacularly threatening entrance. They were there on business, and a greater part of that business was controlling the cacodemons, who were already losing the plot as they began possessing everything from houseplants to alley cats.

Both Zobrondo and Asadak concentrated, drawing in the life force around them and using it to commune with their minions, commanding them to attack humans only. To enter their bodies and subjugate their spirits, crushing down any iota of humanity.

Cry havoc and let slip, the cacodemons of hell.

Brother turned on brother, sister on sister. Neighbors attacked each other with anything at their disposal.

And those who had not been possessed ran screaming, not knowing where to run to, just simply running.

It was a sight to warm Zobrondo's heart.

Or it would have been, if had one.

A few of the more industrious possessed had gone pyro and were torching shops and motor vehicles. Others were smashing everything they could see. But mainly it was a case of the possessed attacking either each other, or any non-possessed human.

An absolute living nightmare of a situation.

Zobrondo turned to his compadre and was in mid-gloat when the first blessed round struck him in the shoulder.

A spray of black blood blossomed from the wound and the demon lord staggered sideways.

'Shit,' he screamed. 'They're here. I've been struck by a bolt of holy fire.'

Asadak, who was marginally less cowardly than his taller compatriot, glanced at their attackers.

'Hold on,' he shouted. 'That's not an Archangel. It's just a bunch of old farts with firearms.'

Zobrondo stopped wailing. 'Well how come I've been so direly wounded?'

Asadak looked at the wound and shook his head. 'It's barely a scratch,' he said. 'They've probably coated their ammunition with holy water or something. It'll hurt, but they can't kill us. It really isn't a problem.'

Another round struck Zobrondo. This one in the chest, knocking the breath out of him.

Then one hit Asadak in the posterior.

'Crap,' he squealed. 'I been shot in the butt.'

'Thought you said it really wasn't a problem,' noted Zobrondo.

'That was when you were being shot. Me being shot is most definitely a problem.'

'Well let's get out of the way and get some of the cacodemons to attack those old assholes,' suggested Zobrondo as he ran for cover.

Asadak hobbled after him and they slipped behind a large SUV.

Then both of them turned their attention to every cacodemon and possessed human within sight, and with a burst of physic energy, compelled them to attack the heavily armed geriatrics that made up the Hartrock's annual town fair committee.

Suddenly, Zobrondo burst out laughing.

'What?' enquired Asadak.

'I just got it,' chuckled the taller demon lord. 'You got shot in the ass. You got ass attacked. As-adak. Get it?'

'Fuck you,' snapped Asadak. 'That's not funny.'

'It is,' disagreed Zobrondo. 'It so is.'

Chapter 39

Esme took a bead and pulled the trigger. The high velocity round struck the possessed Hartrock resident in between his eyes, blowing his brains out the back of his head.

'Take that, you face munching veggie pervert,' she yelled.

'You just shot Pete Barton,' yelled father Evans, his voice only marginally shy of complete hysteria.

'Yep, sure did,' agreed Esme.

'In the head,' continued father Evans. 'Why? Maybe we could have saved him.'

'No way,' argued Esme. 'The silly ass was eating people's faces. There's no coming back from that.'

'Now who's going to judge the humorous vegetable contest?' raved the preacher.

Esme shrugged. 'No idea. But I know it won't be Pete.'

'Harsh, but true,' agreed Lizzy as she pulled off a quick double tap, taking out another possessed maniac.

Father Evans was trying a different tack, one more fitting to a man of God. Instead of simply killing any of the possessed, he was attempting to drive the cacodemons from them.

He had gone full exorcist.

The only problem being, whenever he cast holy water upon them and commanded the possessor leave their human host, the holy water did such a number on the possessee that even when the cacodemon was driven out, the human host died from the horrific burns the holy water had inflicted on them.

'Father, if I could make a suggestion,' ventured Clive. 'To me it seems like whatever it is you are doing, is not helping. All that's happening is you're causing terrible pain to folk, with no actual up side. Rather you just beat them to death with that there brass crucifix of yours, or step aside and let us shoot them.'

Father Evans backed off, accepting the fact that he could not save any of the dementated townsfolk, but unable to bring himself to purposely kill them.

The rest of the committee of elders had no such problem, and their weapons barked out with unerring precision.

However, there were well over a thousand insane humans, and the committee had just over a hundred and fifty rounds between them.

You would be amazed how quickly that ammo gets used up.

'I'm out,' announced Esme.

There was a chorus of agreement from all the rest, excluding Lizzy who was on her last two full magazines.

'What now?' questioned father Evans.

'We run,' suggested Clive.

'Don't be ridiculous,' scoffed Esme. 'I got arthritis in both knees and an artificial hip. I haven't moved faster than a walk since the last millennium.'

'What do you suggest?' asked Clive.

Esme shrugged as she reversed her grip on her .357 revolver, grasping it firmly by the barrel. 'Still makes a good club,' she noted. 'I reckon all we can do is go down fighting. Father, any last words?'

Father Evans nodded. 'Gather round,' he said softly.

The group moved forwards and stood in front of the preacher who proceeded to flick holy water on them.

'Through this holy anointing may the Lord in his love and mercy help you with the grace of the Holy Spirit. May the Lord who frees you from sin save you and raise you up.'

'Last rites?' asked Esme.

Father Evans nodded.

'Fair enough,' interjected Lizzy as she drew out her Ka Bar. 'Oh well, let's do this. Everyone, it's been a privilege.'

There was a brief round of handshakes, hugging and back slapping, and the geriatric squad walked forth to their last meeting.

Because today was a good day to die.

***

The town of Hartrock burned.

All about lay dismembered human bodies. Some few possessed remained at large, but it was only a matter of time before they too ended up either killing one another, or simply burned to death.

No biggie, their work was done.

Zobrondo and Asadak stood together, skulking behind a low garden wall, hiding from both the sun, and whoever, or whatever may appear.

Basically, they were waiting for the Watchers.

They had been waiting for almost two hours.

And still, nothing.

'I don't think they're coming,' said Zobrondo, his voice tinged with hope and disbelief.

'And I think that you are correct,' concurred Asadak.

'Why?' questioned Zobrondo. 'They always come. They see all. They are the Watchers.'

'And without them…' continued Asadak, leaving the sentence unfinished.

Then the two of them started to laugh. And their mirth grew until they were howling in amusement, relief and pure unadulterated joy.

'The Watchers are gone,' shouted Zobrondo.

'No one to call Michael,' added Asadak.

'Yes,' yelled Zobrondo. 'We are untouchable. We are kings. We are the bee's knees.'

'Yeah,' agreed Asadak. 'Now let's get back to the netherworld and ramp this whole thing up. First, we find out where Brenner is, then we send twenty thousand cacodemons to possess everyone around him. Let's see how he likes that.'

Zobrondo frowned. 'Only problem is, how we going to find him?'

Asadak thought for a moment, then he grinned. 'Don't need to,' he said. 'We just go right on ahead with our plans, raise thousands of cacodemons and mess up a real big town. A city, why not? He will find us, then we stick it to him.'

'Yeah,' agreed Zobrondo. 'Time to get hellacious on his ass.'

Chapter 40

'These magical holographic images aren't working very well,' complained the head of the African Quartet. 'They are fuzzy and almost impossible to see.'

'And I can't hear properly,' added the European leader. 'The sound fades in and out.'

'Firstly,' snapped the Asian boss. 'As I said last time, I will not be a part of any endeavor that uses something as parochial and plebian as Zoom to communicate. We are champions of the universe, not some group of double-glazing salesmen.'

'Even if it's efficient?' questioned the European.

'I wouldn't talk about efficiency,' scoffed the Asian. 'After all, your vaunted, so-called warriors were bested with such ease it makes me wonder if, in fact, you simply sent a gaggle of random civilians off the street. Pathetic.'

'Fuck you.'

'What?' questioned the African leader. 'I can't hear what you are all saying. This holograph sucks. I'm going to use my laptop.'

'No,' shouted the Asian. 'No laptops. Magic. Dark magic. And anyway, we don't have a huge agenda, basically we just need to know why this operation has thus far been a monumental failure.'

'What?' asked the African. 'What's he saying?'

'He said we're all useless,' quipped the European.

'No,' denied the Asian. 'I said *you* were useless. Now please, concentrate. We need to get this under control.'

'I blame Zobrondo,' offered the Russian.

There was a shocked pause.

'I hope that you are not criticizing one of the Dark Lord's most senior servants,' said the Asian.

'Not at all,' blathered the Russian, as he realized he had blundered. 'I only thought that perhaps he could make more use of our warriors and less use of … actually, I'm not sure what he's doing.'

'Exactly,' stressed the Asian. 'And it is not our job to know. Instead, let us look to our own machinations. We have activated all of our agents in the government, entertainment and media. We have opened a line of credit that would run a first world country for a year, but still – nothing.'

'Not strictly true,' argued the Russian. 'We have had numerous sightings of Brenner.'

'Oh, whoop-de-doo,' scoffed the Asian leader. 'Sometimes at the same time at opposite ends of the country. And by the time anyone gets there, he's gone. No, I feel we have tried the carrot, what with a one hundred-million-dollar bounty, now we must add the stick. I feel that we should call on our Dark powers to bring down chastisement and castigation on those who are failing us. A few curses, plague, pestilence and pain shall be visited upon the unsuccessful. What say you all?'

'I approve,' concurred the European.

'How big of you,' sneered the Asian leader. 'The rest?'

There was a general nodding of heads.

'Fine, any suggestions?'

'Who did the committee give the Soul-Linked card to?' enquired the African.

'Some drone called Charles Miller,' replied the Asian. 'Upper-midlevel management in one of the alphabet splinter groups. CIA, NSA, not sure.'

'And I take it his performance has been less than stellar,' noted the African.

'Obviously,' conceded the Asian. 'But then is that his fault, or the fault of the committee?'

'I've never liked that sextet of government approved, fat men,' mumbled the Russian. 'Something about them creeps me out. Their squidgy faces and identical suits. Like they've been cloned out of silly-putty. I say we spread the blame amongst the whole lot. The committee and Miller. Punishments all round.'

'I recommend we go old-school,' said the Russian. 'Something we can do ourselves, without having to call on the Dark Lord himself for assistance.'

'You mean some sort of minor curse?' asked the Asian. 'Like the death of their first born.'

The Russian shrugged. 'Maybe not so drastic at first. I was thinking more, plague of boils. Cover them in carbuncles and pustules. Serious enough to show our displeasure, but not so harsh as to give cause for them to stop working.'

'Allow me to carry out the procedure,' interjected the European.

There was a general murmur of agreement from the other leaders.

'Might as well,' said the Asian leader. 'You got no warriors of any note left. Do have the requisite effects?'

'Yes,' replied the European. 'I have a collection of hair and fingernails as usual. Are you going to contact them to tell them of our displeasure?'

'No. Let them stew for a while first. They will know that it is punishment, and they will know it is from us. After all, they may have been a little ineffectual to date, but they are not stupid.'

'Good, I shall start immediately,' confirmed the European as he cut his connection.

The rest of the magical holograms fizzled into nothingness as the Quartets signed off.

Finally, only the African leader's image hung in the air over the table.

'Umm, anyone,' he said. 'Some help here. How do I turn this stupid piece of magical junk off? Anyone? Anyone? Shit, I told them we should have used Zoom. Anyone? Oh, for fuck's sake.'

***

Miller was weeping.

And not in a controlled adult way. More like a toddler that has just been strapped for stealing his sister's cookie.

Huge, chest heaving, blubbering, snot filled sobs.

'Shut up,' commanded one of the six cabbage patch men seated around the boardroom table opposite Miller. 'Your conduct is both unbecoming and embarrassing.'

'But I'm covered in boils,' sniveled Miller. 'Hundreds of them. And it hurts. And it looks awful.' He let out a cry of pain as yet another suppurating pustule on his face burst with a light pop, covering his chin in dark blood and pus.

'So are we all covered in boils,' snapped the man in the suit. 'We have been cursed. And that is largely due to your absolute and utter incompetence.'

'Am, I going to die,' whimpered Miller.

'Indubitably,' confirmed the man. 'But not from a mere outbreak of pustules. Now, we have gifted you with almost unlimited power, why are you still failing us?'

Miller shrugged and the small movement cause another raft of boils to rupture.

'Let me put it this way. Mister Miller,' continued the cabbage patch man. 'If you do not achieve some measure of successes and bring down Brenner, or at least one of his team in the very near future, I can guarantee the next plague visited on us will not be some minor affliction, it will be life ending. And in the most painful, drawn-out manner possible. Our Dark Lord gives us great rewards, but his treatment of failure is most harsh. Do you understand?'

Miller nodded.

Carefully.

Then he frowned.

'I'm sorry,' he said. 'Dark Lord?'

'It matters not,' responded the man. 'Just do as you are told and you may live a little longer. Now leave.'

And Miller left the room, noting for the first time that he may have made a terrible, terrible mistake when he accepted his current position.

Chapter 41

Hislop had found it more difficult than he expected to collect a mega-team of mercenaries under his umbrella.

The primary reason was due to the fact that there were fewer wars around at the moment, what with Iraq, Afghanistan and most of the African conflicts having drawn to a close. Many of the contractors had moved on, joined private security, bodyguarding or simply left the industry altogether.

So, Hislop ended up with the South African outfit, the Primary Defense Network based in the Bahamas, and a motley collection of ex-European soldiers that called themselves the Caretaker Consortium.

'Gentlemen,' said Hislop. 'Can we bring this meeting to order. Firstly, welcome to all.'

The five men seated at the table, two South Africans, two European officers, and a single representative from the Bahamas outfit, nodded, acknowledging his greeting.

'Secondly,' Hislop hit the lights and projected a montage of photos onto a large screen. Brenner, Solomon, Griff and Suki.

Below the photos, in red print, the figure $100 000 000

'The reason you are here.'

There was an audible intake of breath from the contractors sitting at the table. Hislop hid his grin. He knew he had them now.

'Hey, guy,' stated the South African, his voice deep, accent guttural. Inherently aggressive.

'Yes,' responded Hislop.

'Is that Ded Brenner?'

'Actually, it is,' concurred Hislop.

Both of the South Africans closed their laptops and stood up.

'You could have saved us all a lot of time and aggravation if you'd just told us that in the first place,' said the boss man.

'What do you mean?'

'I mean, no one takes on that guy,' replied the South African. 'You do know, he's not even human?'

'Look, I acknowledge, he comes with some serious back stories,' admitted Hislop. 'But he's just a man. A well trained one, I give you. And of course, there is the one hundred million dollars.'

'You didn't hear me,' snapped the South African. 'I said he isn't human. Not, he doesn't seem human.'

'What exactly do you mean by that?' asked Hislop.

The South African laughed. 'If you don't know, guy,' he replied. 'You are in for one huge shock. I bid you goodbye.'

'What about the money?' yelled Hislop at them as they left.

'Dead men don't get to spend money,' replied the South African as he closed the door behind the two of them.

Hislop frowned, unsure what to say to the three men sitting opposite him.

'We are still in,' stated Hans, the German operative. 'Although I must say, I have worked with Colonel Botha before, and if he is not prepared to go up against this Brenner character, I believe we should proceed with caution.'

'But you are still willing to commit,' affirmed Hislop.

Hans shrugged. 'Our combined operations are much stronger together. And one hundred million can stretch far. There is enough for everyone, and we stand a better chance of success working together. So, yes, we are all in.'

The Bahamas man nodded.

'Excellent,' said Hislop as he turned to Godfrey who was sitting in the corner of the room, his briefcase on his lap, hands folded together on top of it. 'Godfrey, tell us what intel you have gathered thus far.'

The accountant stood up, cleared his throat and stepped forward. 'Actually, for someone who is wanted by literately every alphabet agency, the police, the Pentagon, the army, and most private contracting firms, mister Brenner is proving to be exceptionally illusive.

'Well, let me clarify that statement. He has actually been spotted many times, however, often at the same time period and in different parts of the country, many, many miles apart.'

'I don't get it,' admitted Hans.

Godfrey nodded. 'Exactly. Neither do we. However, our sources have picked up something that may prove to lead somewhere. Have you ever heard of the Quartet?'

Hans nodded. 'Rumors. Not much more than that. A shadowy elite, something like the Illuminati. I would dismiss it out of hand, but a soldier I worked with once was rumored to have joined them. Whatever, I never heard of him again. So, either he did join some super-secret society, or he died in some miserable shithole in Africa somewhere and just disappeared. Whatever, he was good. One of the best I ever knew. Why, what have they got to do with Brenner?'

'I can't be one hundred percent sure about this,' answered Godfrey. 'But it appears they are the ones who instituted the massive bounty on his head.'

'I heard it was the CIA,' argued Hans. 'Well, some American government agency or other.'

'As I said, I can't be sure. It just seems they are involved.'

'Well, that doesn't help us at all,' interjected Hans. 'We need eyes on in order to take him down.'

'True, but any intel is good intel,' countered Godfrey. 'However, there is more. Obviously, the sightings of Brenner thus far are either false, or he has a way of travelling almost instantaneously across vast distances, or there are more than one of him.

'Whatever the actual facts are,' continued the accountant. 'We need to be ready to intercept the next sighting. To that end, I have rented us a V-22 Osprey tilt rotor aircraft. It's fast and capable of VTOL. We stay alert, and the moment we hear of a sighting, we run hard.'

Hans nodded. 'It's a plan,' he admitted. 'Not a great plan, but the best we can do for now. I'm in.'

'As are we,' interjected the leader of the Bahama's outfit, speaking for the first time.

Good,' said Hislop. 'Get your men ready and Godfrey will take you all to our camp.'

He watched the men leave and sighed. It wasn't quite what he had hoped for. But still, at least he had a team of over thirty, top-flight, veteran soldiers that he considered to be more than capable of taking on Brenner and his team of misfits.

It was now only a matter of time.

Chapter 42

'Man, this town is well and truly messed up,' said Griff.

The team were wandering through the burning town of Hartrock, Wyoming.

Griff had picked up a lot of black ops chatter on the dark net, as well as a raft of encrypted communications that he had broken with relative ease. It was all regarding an extinction level event in the town of Hartrock.

They had piled into the Winnebago and travelled straight there, driving through the night.

The entire area was cordoned off, road blocks, Hummers, troop carriers, cops, black Suburbans filled with besuited men, and countless armed guards.

However, Michael had assured them that if they didn't actual run over anyone or cause too much noise, they would remain undetected. As long as they did not venture too far from him.

Grandma explained to them that it was one of the Archangel's gifts. After all, he often walked the earth, and in order to do so and remain undetected, he had been gifted the power of ultimate stealth. And he could extend this gift to anyone in his group. As well as this, his divine powers even granted Solomon immunity to the sun, as long as he stayed close to the Archangel.

So, Griff had parked the Winnebago on the outskirts of the town, and the team walked on in.

Max was still walking around with an expression of near rapture on his face as he struggled to come to grips with the fact, he was teamed up with no less than three angels. And that he was their conduit to the Lord. The knowledge filled him with both awe and faith.

As they neared the town center, there were less men-in-black, and military, and more people wearing full Hazmat suits.

Dead bodies lay scattered about with casual abandon. Most were torn to pieces, as if ravaged by wild animals.

Griff stopped to inspect one of the dismembered corpses.

'Look here,' he pointed at a couple of the wounds. 'Those are human teeth marks. And if you look closely at their teeth, you can see pieces of human skin and flesh. These dudes basically ate each other.'

'What in God's name would cause them to do that?' gasped Max.

'Not God's name,' interjected Michael. 'Beelzebub. This is the dark one's doing.' The Archangel sniffed the air. 'Demons,' he stated. 'At least one, maybe two demon Lords, and many, many cacodemons. This was a serious intrusion. The worst I have seen for centuries. Perhaps even millennia.'

'We've come up against these demon dudes before,' said Brenner. They attacked a few towns a while back. They didn't prove to be much of a problem. Basically, we just beat them to a pulp, problem solved.'

'What did they look like?' asked Michael.

'Short, pot bellies, dark gray almost black rubbery skin. Thin little arms and legs. Loads of teeth,' answered Griff.

'Those were mere Quasits,' scoffed Michael. 'Barely demons at all. They are the hellish equivalent of an imp. A mischievous entity at best.'

'Yeah, well, they sure had the ability to fuck shit up,' argued Griff. 'The little assholes killed loads of innocent people.'

'I'm sure,' accepted Michael. 'But compared to the cacodemon, they are as naught. The cacodemon's main power is possession. They have the ability to enter a human's soul and subjugate it. Turning the human into a mere ravaging beast that seeks only to kill and destroy. They are they vilest of creatures.'

'Where are they now?' asked Brenner.

'On the death of their host, they return to the nether hells,' answered Michael.

'So how do you kill them?' continued Brenner.

'That's the problem,' said Michael. 'Technically, they are more wraith than substantial being. Not entirely made of flesh, so they are very hard to kill. The most efficient way to dispose of them is to exterminate the host, thus banishing the cacodemon back to hell.'

'Unacceptable,' snapped Brenner. 'If this happens again, we will not stand idly by waiting for crowds of innocents to be possessed just to make it easier to get rid of the demons. We need to off the little SOB's before they start with their wholesale possession racket.'

'And as an aside,' interjected Solomon. 'If you haven't seen this level of incursion for ages, why now?'

Michael scowled in an effort to cover his embarrassment, but he refrained from answering.

'The Watchers normally stop this from happening,' said Grandma. 'They see it happening, then they would call Michael or one of the other Archangels who in turn would close the portal and drive the demon lords back to hell.'

'I see,' mused Solomon. 'But as laughing boy here has pissed off the Watchers to such an extent, they no longer wish to be a part of the great game, we're now all well and truly up shit's creek sans paddle.'

'It's not my…' began Michael. Then he stopped and his face dropped. 'It is my fault,' he admitted. 'Woe,' he cried. 'Great misfortune have I brought upon this world. And lo, do I repent and pray for punishment. Rend my bones, Lord. Tear my hair and rain down holy fire on me.'

'Hey, slow down,' snapped Brenner. 'We've all made mistakes, dude. Just suck it up and make a plan. And you,' he continued as he turned to face Griff who was using his divine invisibility to pick one of the men-in-black's wallets. 'Stop that. We're on a mission to save humanity, not to steal from shady government officials.'

'Man, I wish I'd had this when I was a teenager,' laughed Griff. 'I would have gained a working knowledge of the female form a hell of a lot sooner than I did.'

Suki rolled her eyes. 'Thank the gods for small mercies,' she said under her breath.

'Michael,' said Grandma. 'You need to focus. How can we predict these incursions, because I would guess that they are more than likely to increase in both size and quantity in the near future?'

'The Watchers are the only beings who could achieve such a feat,' mumbled the Archangel. 'We are all doomed.'

'Come on,' interjected Griff. 'Two old men, and you're saying that you, a freaking Archangel can't do what they did?'

'That is exactly what I am saying,' confirmed Michael. 'Because, firstly, they were not two old men, they were the Watchers, angels of the highest order, and secondly, they could manifest in many places at one time. They were as close to omnipotent as any of us could become.'

'Could we pray for help?' asked Max hesitantly.

'We already did that,' snapped Solomon. 'And we got this useless dipshit,' he finished, pointing at Michael.

'Be very careful, vampire,' warned Michael with a sneer. 'Lest I remove my protection from you and allow the sunlight to scorch the flesh from your bones.'

'Both of you, shut it,' snapped Grandma. 'That's quite enough dick-swinging for now. We need to find the Watchers. Anyone got any ideas?'

No one spoke for a while.

Then Brenner said. 'They always had a penchant for New Orleans. I saw them there a few times. Also, they actually talked about it once or twice. Maybe we should go there, take a look.'

'It's thin,' ventured Solomon. 'But right now, it's all we got.'

'Okay,' said Suki. 'Let's get on the road.'

'Fine,' concurred Brenner. 'Hey, Griff,' he continued. 'Put it back.'

Griff held up a silver hip flask. 'This one had some whisky,' he replied. 'Smells like that smokey Scotch that Solomon likes so much.'

'Laphroaig?' questioned Solomon.

'Yeah, I think so.'

Solomon raised an eyebrow and looked at Brenner.

'Oh hell, sure, why not,' sighed the big man. Keep it. Now, let's get the hell outa Dodge.'

Chapter 43

Mister Reeve smiled broadly.

'What makes you so happy?' enquired mister Bolin.

'I feel terrible,' grinned mister Reeve.

Mister Bolin raised an eyebrow.

'Don't you get it? I think I may have a hangover,' explained mister Reeve.

Mister Bolin frowned. 'Are you sure?'

'Actually, no,' admitted mister Reeve. 'After all, I've never had one before. But it feels like what humans describe.'

'That must mean we are becoming mortal,' concluded mister Bolin. 'How incredible. I am looking forward to our first day as normal human beings. Come, let us go forth into the town and gather new experiences.'

***

Eight hours had passed since the former Watchers had taken to the streets of New Orleans in search of their first human adventure.

Mister Reeve slumped in his chair, sweat streaming down his face, hair plastered to his head. 'I feel terrible,' he mumbled.

'Told you not to eat sixty oysters,' chided mister Bolin. 'You probably got shellfish poisoning or whatever it is that mortals get.'

'I don't think that's an actual thing,' denied mister Reeve.

'Well maybe it's the bottle of tequila you drank.'

'I need some ice-cream,' muttered mister Reeve. 'I think that's what they do. They eat ice-cream.'

'I think they do that when they're upset,' countered mister Bolin. 'Like if they lose a loved one or something. They sit down with a tub of ice-cream.'

Mister Reeve shook his head. 'No, it's definitely when they feel ill. No, wait. Chicken soup. That's it. I need chicken soup. That's for when you're ill. Come on, let's find a restaurant that serves chicken soup.'

The two old men stood up and exited the dive bar on unsteady feet, wobbling precariously into the sweltering New Orleans night.

'Where are we?' asked mister Reeve. 'I don't recognize this part of town.'

Mister Bolin gazed around, taking in the dirty sidewalks, the broken street lights, the potholes and rusted chain-link fencing. 'I feel this may be a little less salubrious than the areas we usually frequent,' he observed.

'There is most definitely a dearth of chicken soup restaurants,' noted mister Reeve.

The two of them continued lurching down the street, feet dragging, heads swiveling drunkenly about.

And then out of the shadows came the bottom feeders. The hyenas that grace those areas where there are two types of people.

The oppressors.

And the victims.

There were six of them. The standard uniform applied, baseball cap on backwards, shades at night, loads of cheap bling, and jail-bait jeans hanging off their skinny butts.

'Hey old man,' sniped the one. The obvious leader marked by the lowness of his jeans and the preponderance of his bling. 'What you all doing out so late?'

The others sniggered. This was primetime material for them. The very acme of wit.

Both mister Reeve and mister Bolin ignored them and continued their less than solid way along the dark street, still scoping for a place that may sell chicken soup.

'Hey,' yelled the head hyena. 'I is talking to you.' He grabbed mister Reeve's collar and spun him around.

Mister Reeve stared at the thug and then shook his head. 'Unhand me, you miscreant, less I destroy you.'

'You couldn't destroy a jelly donut, you creepy old asshole,' snapped the thug. 'Anyhow, fun time is over. Pass over your wallets, jewelry and any other valuables you got. Do it now before I hurt you real bad.'

'No,' replied mister Reeve.

The thug gave no further warning, instead he cocked his right arm and struck mister Reeve a full-blooded blow on his nose.

The sound of the bone breaking was like a booted foot stepping on a gravel path.

Mister Reeve went down like a bolt-shot hog.

Mister Bolin stepped forward and threw a punch at their assailant, but it was slow and uncoordinated, missing by almost a foot.

Laughingly, two of the other lowlifes grabbed the old man by his arms and held him while their chief punched him twice in the face and once more in the gut.

With a final kick, he drove mister Bolin to the floor.

'Not good,' wheezed mister Reeve as he clutched his broken nose. 'After careful contemplation, I have decided that being human sucketh mightily,' he concluded.

'I concur,' admitted mister Bolin. 'However, there is little we can do about it right now.'

'True,' responded mister Reeve. 'But there is one thing for sure, I will not simply give this scum what he wants, as old and ineffectual as I have become, I will not go gently into that good night.'

'Agreed,' replied mister Bolin as he helped his companion to his feet.

'Oh, this is going to be fun,' commented the chief asshole as he drew a switchblade and flicked it open.

He waved the blade in front of him, drawing out the moment, reveling in the sense of power, and then…

His head exploded.

'What the actual fuck,' shouted someone from the shadows. 'Seriously? You went from zero, to head exploding in like under a second?'

Both Reeve and Bolin turned to the voice, as did the shocked thugs that were currently all covered with bits of brain and skull and gore.

'He was going to harm the Watchers,' argued the man who had obviously been responsible for the aforementioned cranial explosion.

'Michael?' asked mister Reeve. 'Is that you? And mister Griff?'

'Yep,' answered Griff. 'The whole team are here,' he gestured to take in Brenner, Solomon, Grandma, Max and Suki. 'We been looking for you.'

The street gang decided that this would be a good time to vacate the immediate premises, what with the obvious introduction of a group of uber-dangerous, head-exploding newcomers changing the entire outlook on what was previously a bit of one-sided violence.

But before they could take their leave, Solomon blurred into movement. A second later, all five were lying on the sidewalk. Some died before they hit the ground, others were clutching feebly at their stomachs as they attempted to stop their insides from becoming their outsides. And one simply lay twitching as his brain tried to work out if he were dead or alive.

Michael shook his head. 'Really? And none of you has anything to say about that? I explode one head and you all get high and mighty with me. But your pet vampire dices five people into separate parts and no one bats an eyelid.'

'Hey, archangel, up yours,' snapped Solomon. 'I ain't nobody's pet.'

Griff simply shrugged. 'What can we say?' he asked. 'It's Solomon.'

Brenner walked up to the two ex-watchers. 'Gentlemen,' he greeted them. 'You both looking a little worse for wear. How's it going becoming human?'

'Honestly,' answered mister Bolin. 'It is not quite the adventure we thought it might be.'

Brenner turned to Michael. 'Is there anything you want to say?'

The archangel knelt before the two old men and held out the half full bottle of ambrosia.

'I humbly apologize for my hubris and my...'

'He's sorry he acted like such an asshole,' interjected Brenner as he took the bottle from Michael and proffered it to mister Bolin. 'Shine?' he asked.

The old man took the bottle with a smile, pulled the cork, took a swig and then passed it to mister Reeve who did the same.

Their injuries healed instantly, the dirt disappeared from their clothes and their eyes once more shone bright with the Holy light.

'That's better,' breathed mister Reeve.

'Gentlemen,' said Brenner. 'We really need to talk.'

Chapter 44

'If you do not stop bowing and scraping and generally acting like some prepubescent teenager who is begging his girlfriend for forgiveness, I may just invoke my powers and turn you into an interesting rock formation somewhere in Colorado,' snapped mister Reeve.

'Yes, Michael,' added mister Bolin. 'We get it. You messed up. However, because you are still one of the most insufferable, egocentric, one track minded, narcissistic beings in the universe, you obviously have no real idea how to apologize. Instead, you settle for humiliating yourself in the misguided belief that somehow this undignified self-debasement will convince us of your genuine desire to turn over a new leaf and become a humble, self-effacing, gentler new Archangel.'

'Not at all…' began Michael.

'Quiet,' insisted mister Bolin. 'I have not finished. Now hear this, and hear it well. You are an ass, Michael. But you need to be an ass. You are God's warrior. The general of his armies. There is no room in you for inner reflection. You are wrath. You are the sword of the Lord. And swords cannot afford to be meek, or humble or diffident. Swords are sharp. They do one thing and one thing only.

'So, enough. We do not forgive you, neither do we place blame. The decision to abscond from our duties was ours alone. And we were wrong. But we figure that one fuckup every twenty thousand years or so is acceptable.

'Enough crawling and pouting, you are an Archangel – act like one.'

'And that is the last any of us will talk about this,' added mister Reeve. 'Now, Brenner, tell us what we have missed.'

Chapter 45

Godfrey pumped his fist in the air.

For the painfully introverted accountant, this was the equivalent of someone else being doing a touchdown dance while shouting *who's your mama?* at the top of their voice.

In other words, Godfrey reckoned he had done good.

He stood up from his desk and went and knocked hesitantly on major Hislop's door.

'Enter.'

The accountant obeyed.

'What?' asked Hislop abruptly, never one to waste words. Particularly on his inferiors.

'I've picked up Brenner and his team,' stated Godfrey. 'CCTV footage from a gas station in New Orleans. Another in the town. Two good hits. They're still there now.'

Hislop grinned. 'Good work, Godfrey,' he said as he took out his cell and hit speed dial. 'Hans. We have Brenner. Wait,

Godfrey will give you the info. I want you in the air in ten minutes. Find him and kill him.'

The colonel handed his cell to Godfrey. 'Dial them in son, let's get this one hundred-million-dollar party started.'

***

'Confidence is high,' yelled the comms expert. 'We have eyes on, multiple hits. I repeat, multiple hits. Operation Brenner is a go. New Orleans.'

Miller came running through. 'Show me.'

The comms expert swiveled his screen. 'There, and there. Just outside of the Lower Ninth Ward, New Orleans.'

Miller squinted at the fuzzy, pixelated images. 'You sure that's him?'

The expert nodded. 'Facial recognition software gives us an eighty seven percent chance. Confidence is high.'

'Who do we have in the vicinity? Heavy hitters.'

'We can call on the local SWAT team, they're pretty much fully under our control. Also, two black ops teams working out of the Marine Corps Support Facility in Federal City.'

'Numbers?'

'Including the SWAT team, I reckon somewhere between forty and sixty.'

'Weapons?'

The expert chuckled. 'Standard SWAT stuff, but the Black Ops boys are armed for bear. Serious ordnance.'

'Contact them ASAP,' ordered Miller. 'Give them the coordinates and keep them posted in real time. Tell them, collateral damage is not a problem. I seriously do not care if they level the whole city. Just get Brenner and his team. Is that clear?'

'Crystal, sir. Termination with extreme prejudice.'

'One more thing,' added Miller.

'Yes, sir?'

'Tell whoever is in command on the ground, if they do not terminate the target, I will personally come down there, rip his eyes out and skull fuck him to death.'

Chapter 46

The team, together with the Watchers, returned to the large suite of rooms in the super-exclusive hotel Solomon had hired.

La Maison Cachée.

A name that literally translated as, The Hidden Hotel.

Situated just across from the St. Louis Cemetery No 1, the oldest cemetery in New Orleans.

Access was gained via a private road tucked in behind the Church of the Ladies of the Cedars of Lebanon.

The unexceptional exterior to the exclusive boutique hotel totally belied the ridiculously sumptuous interior. Marble, Persian carpets, gilded mirrors and genuine Louis XV furniture gave the appearance more of a royal residence than a hotel.

Which was apt, as various royals from around the world oft gathered there.

The suite of rooms the team had booked covered the entire fifth floor, the top floor of the hotel.

They were currently seated around the dining table, drinking shine from the shot glasses mister Reeve had provided.

Mister Bolin sighed. 'We most definitely blundered,' he admitted. 'Perhaps instead of taking such offence at Michael's self-indulgent ravings and leaving our posts, we merely should have punished him and gotten it out of our systems that way.

Griff chuckled. 'You mean like paddled his rear end like a naughty schoolboy?'

Mister Bolin stared at Griff, holding his gaze until the old man looked away. 'No,' answered the Watcher. 'We would not have paddled his rear end like a naughty schoolboy. We would have called down consequential wrath upon him.'

Grandma raised an eyebrow. 'You have that power?'

Both of the Watchers nodded.

'I don't get it,' admitted Brenner.

'Consequential wrath,' repeated Grandma. 'You reap what you sow. Unkindness shall be revisited upon you tenfold. In other words, the vitriol and unkindness Michael put upon them would have been returned on him in spades.'

'How?' asked Brenner.

Grandma shrugged. 'That is not for us to decide. But it is a power gifted to very few. The fact that they could call upon it, and yet they did not, speaks volumes for their self-control.'

Michael dropped to his knees in front of the Watchers once more. 'Again,' he said. 'I beg for forgiveness.'

'As we said before,' answered mister Reeve. 'We do not forgive you, but neither do we place blame.'

'Still…' interjected Michael.

But before he could continue, mister Bolin stood up. 'They come,' he announced. 'From all sides. Many of them.'

'Who? What? Demons? Denizens of hell?' blurted Griff.

Mister Bolin looked at Griff with an expression of such utter disdain that the old man literally cringed.

'What?' asked Griff. 'It's a valid question.'

'People,' responded mister Bolin. 'Armed. Scores of them. I can feel their intent.'

'And what would that intent be?' asked Brenner.

'Death. Yours and all who ride with you.'

'We'll see about that,' snapped the big man. 'Griff, Solomon, Max, go to the Winnebago and tool up. Bring whatever weapons you deem necessary up here. I'm gonna climb onto the roof and see if I can spot anyone.

'I'll come with you,' interjected Michael.

Brenner nodded and everyone started moving.

Except for the Watchers who settled back in their chairs and poured another round of shine.

Ten minutes later. All were once more gathered around the table.

'Couldn't see anything yet,' informed Brenner. 'So if they're on their way, we still don't have line of sight.'

'Cool, we got a bit of time then,' said Griff. 'Hey, you know how to use this?' he continued, asking Max as he held up an M16A1 assault rifle.

'Of course,' affirmed Max. 'I am a Knight of the Holy See. I have received extensive training in all weapons, explosives and unarmed combat.'

'It's yours then.'

Max shook his head. 'I do not mean to be difficult, but I would prefer the M249 Squad Support Weapon.'

Griff chuckled. 'Good choice,' he agreed. 'He handed the SAW over, complete with a two hundred round plastic magazine. 'Anything else take your fancy?'

Max took a Cold Steel machete, four fragmentation grenades, a Colt 45 with three extra magazines and a set of Vietnam era webbing.

Griff nodded his approval. 'Ded?'

The big man shook his head. 'I'll be going wolfman for this,' he said.

'Solomon?' asked Griff.

The man in black also rejected the offer as he extended his talons, like bone-white swords of moonlight.

Suki grabbed a Heckler and Koch UMP in a 45 caliber, and a Colt in the same, plus a few extra magazines for both.

'I think we should move,' said Grandma as she materialized her staff from nowhere. Six feet of polished ebony, topped by a fist sized white crystal that veritably hummed with power. 'If the shit is going to hit the fan, we should see how we can minimize any collateral damage.'

'Suggestions?' asked Brenner.

'The cemetery,' answered Grandma.

'Good idea,' concurred Griff. 'Can't kill dead dudes. I'll climb up top of one of the larger vaults to provide some overwatch.'

'You coming?' Grandma asked the Watchers.

'We will be there, as we need to watch,' they chorused in union.

'Yeah,' murmured Griff. 'I'd forgotten how creepy you dudes can seem. Whatever, let's do this.'

Chapter 47

Specialized Weapons and Tactics, New Orleans division.

Eighteen men under the tactical command of Lieutenant Rock Davidson. The team was split into two groups, Nine in each group. They were currently in the department's two Lenco BearCat armored vehicles.

Sergeant Ronnie Driscoll was in charge of team Omega in BearCat two. Lieutenant Davidson was with team Alpha in BearCat one.

Contrary to what is shown on television, many SWAT members no longer wear the traditional black or blue uniforms, now they tend to look more like the military.

Army green, or camo. Lightweight helmets and ballistic vests. The major difference being their variety of different weapons.

Everything from obscure submachine guns like the FN P90, to M4 carbines and even semi-auto Benelli shotguns.

On their back, emblazoned in yellow, SWAT. Or sometimes merely SHERRIF or POLICE.

They had been informed their target was a rabid right-wing terrorist by the name of Ded Brenner. He had a team of similar fanatical murderous types with him and SWAT were given the go-ahead to take down the enemy with all necessary force.

The police chief made it plain, they were not looking for arrests. They were looking to take out the trash.

***

'We got incoming,' announced Griff from his vantage point atop one of the larger vaults. The old man had linked everyone's cell phones together on an open conference call so they could communicate with ease.

'What?' asked Brenner.

'A pair of armored vehicles. Looks like SWAT.'

'Should I smite them?' enquired Michael.

'Wait,' interjected mister Bolin. 'These are not evil men.'

'How do you know that?' asked Brenner.

Mister Bolin raised an eyebrow but did not deign to answer. 'They are upholders of the law. Protectors of the innocent. This should not be their battle.'

'Dude,' said Brenner. 'I know it's harsh, but if they start trying to kill us, we gotta retaliate. And unfortunately, that retaliation is most likely going to be terminal.'

'Unacceptable,' stated mister Reeve. He turned to Grandma. 'Lamassu, could you subdue them without casualties?'

'Firstly, don't call me that. I gave that name up a thousand years ago, and you know that. And, secondly, obviously, I'm a Malak.'

Both of the Watchers bowed deeply.

'Then please proceed,' said mister Reeve.

***

The two BearCat armored vehicles pulled up at the entrance to the cemetery and the occupants debussed, forming up outside as they did.

Grandma raised her staff, closed her eyes and brought forth her power.

A globe of white light exploded from the tip of the staff and arced through the air to land amongst the SWAT team members, detonating soundlessly in a burst of primary colors.

The effect was instantaneous.

As one, every member's eyes rolled back in their heads, and they sank slowly to the floor.

Unconscious.

Grandma staggered slightly and Brenner had to grab her to prevent her from falling.

'That's me done, folks,' murmured the Malak. 'Takes it out of you, calling on that much power.'

'Really?' asked Solomon. 'But I've seen you do much more. Portals, explosions, all sorts of heavy shit.'

Grandma chuckled. 'Yeah, but that unsubtle crap is easy. You try putting almost twenty full grown men into a state of suspended animation without fucking their brains up for good. Trust me, it's properly difficult. Whatever, don't expect any more from me for at least twenty-four hours. I'm finished.'

'We got more incoming,' warned Griff.

'Numbers?' asked Brenner.

'Shit,' responded Griff. 'Like, all of them. Must be at least ten … no, fifteen black suburbans in a convoy. Like the least subtle undercover dark ops convoy ever. Who do these guys think they're fooling?'

'So, what, forty, fifty dudes.'

'At least,' concurred Griff.

'It's doable,' said Solomon.

'Uh, guys,' interjected Griff. 'South side of the cemetery, another group. Also in SUV's. From what I can see, they don't look government issue. Could be private contractors. Maybe another thirty, maybe a few more.'

'Weapons?'

'Can't tell. But trust me, they'll all be loaded for bear. This does not look good for us.'

'No shit,' sighed Brenner. 'When does it ever?'

Michael smiled as his wings burst from his shoulders, shredding his shirt and exposing his unbelievably well-muscled torso. 'Yes,' he said happily. 'Fight. Time to do battle. We shall vanquish them all with mighty strength of arms.'

With that, he conjured a flaming, six feet long broadsword out of thin air.

Solomon shook his head. 'I can't believe it. I thought Brenner was the king of fucking shit up, now it looks like we've got another one. I really do not deserve this. Seriously.'

'Anyone got a plan?' asked Suki.

Solomon laughed. 'Don't be silly,' he said. 'With Brenner and Michael, the only plan is going to be some minor variation of let's fuck shit up.'

Brenner shrugged. 'True,' he admitted.

'Well, what are we waiting for?' asked Michael. 'It is time to rain down holy fire on the evil doers.'

Brenner exploded into his wolfman form and roared. 'Yeah,' he growled. 'What he said.'

'I'll take the contractors on the South side,' said Solomon. 'Suki, you protect Grandma. Brenner, you and the nutcase angel take the black ops boys. Max, do you think you can find some high ground like Griff and get your SAW to bear on the contractors? Stop them flanking me.'

'What about Brenner and Michael?' asked Max. 'Shouldn't I give them some backup?'

Solomon chuckled. 'Trust me, son,' he said. 'They don't need it. Me, on the other hand, I'm going in solo.'

Max nodded and immediately set off.

Finally, Solomon turned to the Watchers. 'And I suppose, you watch. Griff, cover me, I'm going in.'

Chapter 48

Hislop's contractors arrived in five large SUV's. They pulled up outside the rear entrance to the cemetery and debussed.

Hislop had put Hans in charge of the operation, and although the Bahama outfit wasn't entirely happy, they acceded without much more than a token argument.

'Okay,' said Hans. 'We split into two groups as we enter. Bahama boys go left, me and my boys go right. Last intel puts the target near to the center of the cemetery. We flank them and then hit them together. Wait for my unit to open fire, then you guys join in. Simple, but effective.'

The contactors jogged through the rear gates, splitting up as they did. But before they could go their separate ways, Griff and Max opened fire.

Griff's first shot was bang on target, striking one of the contactors center mass. The man's body armor didn't stop the slug, but it did slow it down enough to save his life. Albeit only for a few more seconds.

Max's initial burst of fire rode high, ricocheting off the roofs of the SUV's. But his second burst drew blood, sending the contractors scurrying for cover behind the various vaults and tomb stones.

'Where's it coming from?' yelled Hans.

'There,' answered Stefan, one of his men. 'Muzzle flashes, eleven …'

Stefan was cut short before he could finish answering, his sentence gurgling to a halt.

'Stefan,' shouted Hans. 'Are you there?'

The incoming fire stopped abruptly. Then a chilling scream rent the night air, followed once again by a wet choking sound, then silence.

'There's something here,' shouted one of the Bahman crew. 'It's…'

This time Hans saw something. An arc of blood against the moonlight, and the hint of movement. Something moving so fast they were a blur in the darkness.

Another scream.

Another thud of a corpse hitting the sod.

Another spray of blood.

Hans saw a severed head roll out from behind a tombstone, an expression of surprise still etched on its face.

Someone fired a long burst on their MP5. 'I got him,' they shouted. 'I swear, I…'

Hans turned on his barrel mounted flashlight, no longer worried about giving his position away to whoever was sniping at them. He was now more worried about the thing that was tearing his men apart.

All about him he could hear men firing, shouting, screaming, running.

But one thing was patently clear. As each second passed, there were less people around him.

Living ones, at any rate.

Slowly, Hans crept forward, sweeping the powerful flashlight from side to side, his finger on the trigger of his MP5.

Blood was everywhere. Like someone had taken buckets of it and splashed it liberally over the vaults and tombstones and memorials. The bodies of the fallen lay scattered amongst the vaults. Most of them had their throats cut. Many had lost their heads.

The stench of death was thick in the night air. The sickly-sweet smell of blood coated the back of Han's throat, making him want to gag.

Then there was a blur of movement.

And he was lying on his back, his weapon nowhere near him, his right arm twisted at an impossible angle, shards of bone poking through his jacket.

Above him stood a pale man in a back suit. His face and hands covered in gore.

The man smiled; his extended canines shockingly white against the deep crimson coating of blood.

'I figured you for the leader,' the man said. 'So, I left you until last. Question time, who do you work for?'

'Fuck you.'

'Now that's not nice,' said the man. 'Impolite and unnecessary. Tell you what, you cooperate, and I shall kill you quickly. If not, you will see the sun rise. But you will wish you hadn't. Clear?'

Hans nodded. 'I am a private contractor. There were two teams, separate businesses. We got together for the bounty. That's it. Nothing more to tell. I swear.'

'I believe you,' said the man in black. 'Oh, one more thing, do you know where Shadow is being held?'

Hans's expression of puzzlement was obviously genuine. He shook his head.

He didn't see the blow that killed him.

Solomon had been true to his word, and the contractor died instantly.

Then the man in black turned and headed towards Brenner and Michael, ready to give them a hand if need be.

Chapter 49

The problem with most black ops units is they tend to work in small groups. Two, three or maybe four members.

What they do not do very much, if at all, is arrive *en masse*, fifty plus strong and launch an all-out assault.

However, sometimes needs must, and they had been tasked with taking out this specific group and to hell with the consequences.

The entire convoy debussed and headed towards the center of the cemetery. At least three operations personal were getting real time updates via their comms units, directing them towards their target.

'Right, gentlemen,' said Tod Kowalski. A member of the National Clandestine Service (NCS). 'I suggest we break into our standard groups and attempt to surround the targets.'

'Who put you in charge, Kowalski?' asked Peter Harper. Central Intelligence Agency (CIA).

'I'm the ranking officer.'

'Says who?'

Kowalski shook his head. 'I am a captain, that outranks you, Harper.'

'No, it doesn't. How could it, CIA don't have ranks, we got pay grades. And how can you compare my grade to your rank?'

'Technically, I think I outrank both of you,' interjected Rebecca Hofmann. 'I'm a special agent, Homeland Security. I'm pretty sure that's higher than a captain or a whatever pay grade you are, Harper.'

'No way,' argued Kowalski. 'Special agent is equivalent to a sergeant. A captain would be an assistant special agent in charge.'

Before the group of would-be-leaders could continue their argument, another one of the black ops team yelled out.

'Umm, sir, ma'am,' interjected one of the operatives. 'Is that the SWAT team? There, on the floor.'

Kowalski turned to look. 'Holy shit,' he murmured. 'What the hell happened to them?'

'Hey, what is that?' yelled another operative, his voice pitching high in panic.

Everyone turned to look.

Approaching them was an impossibility.

Walking calmly amongst the gravestones, a humanoid figure. Perhaps six feet six, two hundred pounds. Jeans, shirtless, his musculature ripped to the point of near ridiculousness.

From his back flared a pair of wings, fully thirty feet in span.

All about him glowed an ethereal light.

And in his right hand he held a six foot long, flaming broadsword.

He stopped some twenty yards from the group.

And then he smiled.

It was an expression of such beauty, such exquisite loveliness that it caused most of the group of operatives to catch their breath.

Then the otherworldly being spoke, its voice like the ringing of trumpets. And thusly it spake unto them.

'And vengeance shall be mine, sayeth the Lord. And lo, did he cry havoc and call upon his great captain to weigh their souls. And he did find them wanting. And thus did the leader of the heavenly hosts rain down great wrath and holy fire upon them.'

Kowalski shouldered his M16, drew a bead and cranked off the entire thirty round magazine on full auto.

Every round struck the glowing apparition center mass.

Michael frowned.

That was all. He did not flinch, nor stagger backwards, nor give any other recognition to the fact he had just been hit by thirty full metal jacket, high velocity rounds capable of taking down a bull elephant.

'Oh, shit,' breathed Kowalski.

And then Brenner roared as he joined the fray, leaping from the top of one of the vaults, to land in the middle of the group of operatives.

At the same time, Michael attacked, sweeping his flaming sword through all who stood before him.

Some of the less brave turned and ran. Or at least they attempted to, but as they did, Max and Griff cut them down with a fusillade of lead.

The rest of the group opened fire. Thousands of rounds filled the air, grenades were thrown, and tracers stitched an intricate pattern in the New Orleans night sky.

It was a tossup as to which of the supernatural beings were the most terrifying.

Brenner, dark, all tooth and claw and blood. A nightmare come to life.

Or Michael, all ethereal light and smiles and uninhibited laughter. A being truly enjoying his work. Ecstatic to deliver the Lord's vengeance to the evil doers. An angel with a mission.

However, after a few minutes of observation, the award as to most frightening entity went to Brennerwolf. Not because his kills seemed to be a trifle more bloody, more visceral, primeval and gory.

No, it was because before each kill he would drag the enemy close and ask the same question, his voice devoid of emotion. Chillingly calm.

Unnaturally so.

'Where is Shadow?'

Each and every time he paused to repeat the question, an operative took the opportunity to shoot him, or stab him, or throw a grenade in his direction.

But it did not deter the wolfman in the slightest.

Again, and again and again he asked.

'Where is Shadow?'

And then, there was no one left to question.

Brennerwolf threw his head back and howled.

Every animal in the city responded. A cacophony of barks and growls and whine and squeals and shrieks. Like every creature in the area had simultaneously gone mad with grief.

Michael put his hand on the wolfman's shoulder. 'I'm sorry, Ded,' he said. 'But have faith, we will find her. Whatever it takes.'

'Oh yeah,' snarled Brenner. 'What about the grand plan?'

Michael grimaced. 'I said, whatever it takes,' he affirmed.

'Thank you, Michael,' growled Brenner softly.

'Hey dudes,' called out Griff as he jogged up, running next to Solomon. 'You guys came, you saw and you kicked some ass. Nice work.'

Solomon looked at the devastation around him and shook his head. 'Did you have to destroy so many vaults?' he asked. 'I mean, look, that one's Nicholas Cage's mausoleum.' He pointed at a pyramid shaped marble structure that stood around ten feet high. Well, it used to be ten feet high. Right now, it was rather truncated, the top having been blown off by a random hand grenade.

'Man,' said Griff. 'Nicky's gonna be pissed. I wouldn't want to be in your shoes when he finds out you fucked up his vault.'

'Well, we just won't tell him,' snapped Brenner.

Grandma appeared out of the darkness with Suki, Max and the Watchers.

'You boys okay?' she asked.

Brenner nodded.

'Holy crap,' cussed Grandma. 'What the hell have you done to Nicky's tomb?'

'It wasn't me,' argued Brenner. 'It was those CIA douches. I got nothing to do with it. Jeez, you guys act like I personally blew the fucking thing up. Anyhow, he's not dead yet, he can get it fixed up.'

'Wow,' said Grandma. 'Just, wow. Look, we'd better move out, and fast. This place is going to be crawling in Feds soon.'

Brenner nodded his agreement as he morphed back into human mode, grabbing his rucksack from Suki and pulling on jeans and a t-shirt. 'Griff, get the Winnebago and bring it to the rear entrance. Let's move.'

Chapter 50

Colonel Hislop keyed his comms unit again. But as before, no response.

He had been in contact with Hans, and then the airwaves were full of shouts and gunfire and finally, screams of unmitigated terror.

And then only static.

He stood up from his chair and walked through to Godfrey's office.

'Do you have eyes on?' he asked.

Godfrey shook his head. 'Only marginally. Here,' he turned his computer screen to face the colonel. 'This is some enhanced CCTV footage from a hotel across the street from the cemetery. You can't see much, but you can see enough.'

Hislop watched the scenario unfold.

It was impossible to tell exactly what was happening, bar the fact that his men were dying.

Quickly.

The footage was out of focus, and whatever was attacking the contractors was obviously not human.

Because nothing human could move that fast.

In literally two minutes, the attack was over. All his men dead.

'Was that Brenner?' he asked.

Godfrey shook his head. 'Look,' he hit a few keys, enhancing the footage and pausing it.

A blurred image coalesced on the screen.

Pale face, fangs, a dark suit.

'It seems to be his compatriot,' noted Godfrey. 'Solomon something or other.'

'Where is Brenner?'

Godfrey tapped away for a few seconds and another set of images scrolled across the screen.

'It seems as if someone else attacked our targets at the same time. From the other side of the cemetery,' informed Godfrey. 'Brenner and some other members of his team went to dispatch them.'

'So, you are telling me that a single man took out over thirty well-armed, highly trained contractors in just over a minute?'

'I'm not sure Solomon is a man. I mean, he does not appear to be human. But ostensibly, yes. That is what happened.'

'And the people who took on Brenner, how did they fare?'

Godfrey shook his head. 'Sixty plus operatives. All dead, from what I can tell.'

'This is some seriously screwed up shit,' said Hislop.

'Yes,' agreed the accountant.

Hislop sighed. 'What is the balance in the company account?'

'Around two million, sir.'

'Good,' said Hislop, as he drew his Glock pistol and shot Godfrey in the temple. 'Enough for me to have a new start, not enough for two.'

Pushing Godfrey's corpse off his chair, Hislop sat down and accessed the company bank.

'Time to transfer this into my personal account,' he muttered to himself as he keyed in the sixteen-digit password.

But instead of gaining access, the computer beeped and a warning flashed up.

Password incorrect. Please try again.

Hislop frowned and retyped the numbers, pressing each key slowly and deliberately so as not to make a mistake.

The computer beeped once more.

But this time, instead of asking him to try again, a new message filled the screen.

Dear colonel Hislop. If you are reading this message then fuck you very much your thieving murderous piece of shit. May you rot in hell.

With little respect and no affection whatsoever. Godfrey.

P.S. Fuck you even more.

Hislop sank back into the chair, an expression of utter devastation on his face. 'Oh, well played, you little shit,' he murmured. 'Well played indeed.'

***

Miller sat with a group of comms experts. They were relaying the attack on Brenner's team in real time. High-def satellite footage viewed on a gigantic LED screen.

The same visual was overlaid with sound being transmitted from one of the SWAT officers, and various black ops members.

It wasn't quite like watching a movie, but it was close.

'There they go,' noted Miller. 'The SWAT team will get there first.'

The feeling in the room was upbeat. Almost jubilant. This hit had been a long time coming. And now, with an entire SWAT team, plus a further specialist black ops group, it went without saying – Brenner and his friends were dead meat.

'SWAT are debussing now,' commented one of the comms experts. 'Forming up. Wait… what the fuck? SWAT team are down, I repeat SWAT team are down.'

'How?' yelled Miller. 'Ordnance type?' he questioned, even though he was watching the exact same picture as the analysts.

'Umm … some sort of light?' ventured one.

'Are they dead?' asked Miller.

'Unclear, sir. But they are not moving.'

'I didn't hear anything,' said Miller. 'They just hit the deck.'

'The black ops people have arrived,' announced one of the analysts.

'I can see that,' snapped Miller, who was feeling decidedly less upbeat than he had before his entire SWAT team simply fell down.

'Black ops deploying.'

'Give me sound,' commanded Miller.

The room listened for a few seconds.

'Are they seriously arguing about who outranks who?' asked Miller incredulously. 'Can you patch me through to one of them so I can tear them a new asshole.'

The comms expert was about to comply when the shit hit the fan.

Everyone in the room leaned forward in their chairs. Some, like Miller, actually stood up.

'Hey, what is that?' he yelled, perfectly mimicking the operative on the ground.

No one answered.

'I said, what is that?' repeated Miller. 'Come on guys, I got wall-to-wall experts here, give me some actionable intel.'

'An angel?' questioned one of the experts.

'Don't be stupid,' snapped Miller. Although, to be fair, he thought, the SOB is glowing, he has wings and he's carrying a damn burning sword.

Then Brenner entered the fray.

'Oh, for fuck sakes,' yelled Miller, who was fast becoming some serious competition to Rufus 'Fucking' Johnstone, as his bafflement overrode his ability to form cogent sentences without a cuss word. 'What the fuck is that?'

The same expert who had voiced his opinion regarding angels answered hesitantly. 'A werewolf?'

No one gainsaid him.

Because whatever anyone actually thought or believed, there was no denying that what they were looking at was most definitely a werewolf.

Three minutes later all of the operatives were dead.

There was a stunned silence.

Then someone said. 'Is that Nicholas Cage's vault? Man, those guys totally messed it up.'

Miller didn't react.

He had failed.

Utterly, undeniably and absolutely.

With a grunt of agony, he felt the full weight of the curse hit him. The cabbage-patch men had warned him, you fail us this time, you will suffer the consequences.

Within seconds, Miller's entire body was covered in huge suppurating pustules.

Ten seconds after that, his flesh began to liquefy and slide off his bones.

He didn't even have time to scream.

Although many of the people in the room did.

And they shrieked in absolute horror. Lustily and heartily at the tops of their lungs as their erstwhile boss disintegrated in front of them, filling the room with the stench of brimstone and rotting flesh.

And the sound of demonic laughter filled the air as the contact was sealed.

Another soul was dragged down to hell.

The deal done.

And just like that, Miller's cameo was over.

A tale told by an idiot, full of sound and fury, signifying nothing.

Chapter 51

'Tents.' Sighed Solomon. 'Is this really the best you could do?'

'It's the best way to stay undercover,' replied Griff. 'The trees should do a good job of concealing us from satellites, we're off the beaten track, and all of my comms are scrambled to the point that the NSA couldn't listen in even if they knew where I was.'

'Yeah but, tents,' repeated the man in black. 'No room service, no aircon.'

After the battle, they had boarded the Winnebago and Griff had hightailed it north, driving deep into the De Soto National Forest.

He figured it was time to go deep, deep under cover and reassess their options.

Everyone had agreed, bar Solomon who figured it was better to hide in plain sight, preferably in a five-star hotel.

Obviously, he had been outvoted.

And to be fair, Griff had gone for the very best when he had prepared for the eventuality of having to camp for a short while. Four, large inflatable Coleman tents, each large enough to comfortably sleep four. Combined with deluxe inflatable airbeds and the Winnebago kitchen, they were hardly in the realms of roughing it.

Solomon and Suki got one tent. Griff allocated another for Grandma and himself, Brenner, Max and Michael took the third and the Watchers got the last one.

'I'll fix some dinner,' volunteered Suki while Griff and Max set up camp.

'I'm going wolf for a bit,' announced Brenner. 'Going to scout around. Be a couple of hours.'

The Watchers watched, because that is what they do.

Michael had never seen an inflatable tent before and was genuinely impressed.

'How marvelous,' he stated. 'A pump-up dwelling. Ingenious.'

'Don't suppose you wanna help,' quipped Griff.

Michael shook his head, the obvious sarcasm completely lost on him. 'No thank you,' he answered. 'I will continue to spectate.'

Later that evening, Brenner returned to find Solomon, Michael, Suki and the Watchers sitting around a fire drinking shine.

'Where's Griff,' he asked.

'In the Winnebago with Max,' answered Suki. 'Doing some research. Been at it since you left.'

The big man walked over to the RV and let himself in.

Max was on an encoded satellite phone.

Griff was at his bank of computers.

'Hey, Ded,' he greeted. 'See anything worth reporting?'

Brenner shook his head. 'And you?'

'Well, Max here has been burning up the airways to Italy. Been jabbering away in Italian for the last hour. Not sure what he's doing. But I got nothing new.'

'Shadow?'

Griff grimaced. 'No, sorry my friend. I contacted everyone in my network. Maybe Max has had some luck.'

At that moment, Max disconnected his call. 'I do have some information,' he announced. 'Not about your lady, but who knows, it may provide us with a lead.'

'Tell me,' said Brenner.

'It appears that the power behind all that is happening is an ancient international group called the Quartet.'

'Oh, those fuckers,' interjected Griff. 'Nah, we took them out last year. Well, Solomon did. Blew up an entire hotel in Vegas to get them.'

Max shook his head. 'No, you took out the American branch. There are four more, Europe, Asia, Russia, Africa. Each region had a Quartet controlling it. I have just been talking to Cardinal Angelo Sandri, and he told me reliable informants have confirmed the Quartet put the money up for Brenner's assassination.

'They also have great power over governments, the military, big business and the media. Beyond doubt they are the most powerful group in the world. When people talk about the Illuminati, the Quartet is what they actually envisage.'

'We've taken them down before, we can do it again,' stated Brenner.

'Well, there's more,' admitted Max. 'Cardinal Sandri says the Knights of the Holy See have discovered that the Quartet are in fact a dark cabal. Many of them are hundreds of years old, gaining longevity and power through their worship of the Father of Lies.'

'So, devil worshippers,' noted Griff.

'Loosely speaking, yes,' confirmed Max. 'However, in a case like this it goes much deeper. They are not mere worshippers; they are a part of his unholy collective. More favored servants than simple followers. These are very powerful beings. However, there is more.

'The various Quartets have dispatched their finest assassins to kill you. Apparently, you have already bested one of their cadres. The European force.'

'Must have been those dudes in Vegas,' said Brenner. 'Didn't sweat them. They weren't so bad.'

'Nevertheless,' continued Max. 'There are three more cadres, and the Cardinal urges you to take their threat seriously.'

'Fine, consider it taken seriously,' quipped Brenner.

Max hesitated.

'What?' asked the big man. 'Come on, spit it out.'

'Well, the Cardinal has given me the suspected location of the cadres. He was hoping that you would be able to dispatch them. They are evil men, and deserve retribution to be visited upon them.'

Brenner nodded. 'Took you long enough to get to the point, boy,' he said. 'Obviously we'll take care of them. After all, they may have info regarding Shadow. Give, where are they?'

'They're in an area called Mount Marlon.'

Griff tapped at his keyboard. 'Hey, that's close to Shadow's clan. We can get them to scout the area while we drive up there.'

'Can you get them on the line?' asked Brenner.

Griff shrugged. 'Not sure. You know they tend to be a bit shy of technology. Rufus 'Fucking' Johnstone might still have the cell we gave him. But I doubt he's kept it charged. I can give it a go.'

The old man took out his encrypted cell and dialed.

'It's ringing,' he said as he turned on the speaker so all could hear, and then placed the phone on the desk.

After six or seven rings, someone answered.

'Who the fuck is this?'

'Hey, Rufus, it's Brenner.'

'Oh, fuck, sorry boss,' apologized Rufus. 'Just that no one has phoned this fucking thing since I last spoke to Griff a year ago.'

'So how come you keep it charged?' asked Griff.

There was an embarrassed pause. Finally, Rufus answered. 'Because I fucking play Candy Crush.'

'Really? How sweet.'

'Fuck you, Griff. Anyway, boss, what you want?'

Brenner told him.

'I'll get everyone scouting the area,' confirmed Rufus. 'What's your ETA?'

'Late tomorrow evening,' confirmed Brenner. 'See you then.'

'Fucking A, boss.'

Brenner rang off. 'Right, let's catch everyone up, eat and get some shuteye. Early start tomorrow.'

Chapter 52

Shadow had no idea how long she had been incarcerated.

She had attempted to keep some sort of track of time by marking the wall each time she was fed.

But after ten marks, a team of demons had come into her cell and, using pitchforks they had destroyed her markings and covered the rest of the walls in so many scratches she was no longer able to keep a visible track.

And sometimes they would give her two meals only an hour apart, then not feed her for what felt like thirty or forty hours.

It was all done to break her spirit.

To crush her will.

The tactics were not working.

In fact, Shadow was stronger now than she had been during her first few days in the dungeon.

Daily meditation and physical exercise had sharpened her senses and honed her instincts.

And now, despite the obvious magical restraints that covered her, she was almost able to bring forth her mountain lion spirit.

Almost.

She finished the bowl of gruel, licking it clean in order to get every ounce of possible nourishment, and then she sat cross legged and delved deep into her soul.

Show me the lion, she commanded.

Bring me the beast.

Chapter 53

It was a tribute to both Griff's driving skills and the remarkable upgrades to the Winnebago's suspension that the old man was able to follow the dirt track all the way to the Mountain Lion clan.

They debussed to be greeted by alpha Kobach and Rufus 'Fucking' Johnstone.

Both of them dropped to one knee in front of Brenner, waiting for him to acknowledge them.

There had been a time, a few years before, when the big man would have been embarrassed by such a display. But eventually he had come to accept the fact that he was the Alpha of all Alpha's, and that was simply the way other shifters would behave around him.

To insist they did not would be to belittle them.

'Rise, my friends,' he greeted them. 'And thank you for allowing us into your territory.'

'Our territory is yours, Great Wolf,' returned Kobach as he stood.

The two of them hugged.

'Good to see you, big man,' said the lion alpha.

Rufus also stepped forward and threw his arms around Brenner. 'How the fuck are you, Boss? Holding up?'

Brenner shrugged. 'Any news about Shadow.'

'If there was, don't you think we would have fucking told you,' said Rufus. 'Umm … with all due respect, boss.'

Brenner grinned ruefully. 'True, sorry. I just worry all the time.'

'They will not do her any harm,' interjected Kobach. 'I am not sure of the where's and why's of the issue, but if they had meant to harm her, they would already have done so. And they would have informed us in order to bring hurt to you.

'Now come, let us eat, and we will tell you what our scouts have discovered.'

***

As was Brenner's usual *Modus Operandi*, the best time to do something was as soon as possible. And the best way to overcome any obstacle was through the use of overwhelming force.

Or as Griff put it, by fucking shit up.

Mount Marlon was some eighteen miles away from the clan seat. To a shifter in full lion mode, that is a mere ten minutes travel at full sprint, their top speed approaching eighty miles an hour.

Brenner and Solomon could travel the distance in just over half that time.

Rufus had informed them there were at least thirty Quartet warriors, plus another twenty or so staff. Cooks, armorers, general servants and the like.

Even the servants were heavily armed at all times.

The werelion had watched them train and he begrudgingly admitted they were good.

Very good.

'It's like they have some otherworldly powers,' he noted. 'Definitely stronger than a normal human. Faster, more aggressive.'

'I didn't find them to be so bad,' said Brenner.

'Yeah, well maybe you got the fucking B-team,' argued Rufus. 'Trust me when I say, these dudes are not to be taken lightly.'

As a result of Rufus's observations, Brenner had gone for what he considered overkill.

Himself, Solomon, and Michael would breach the house while Max and Griff acted as overwatch, sporting long guns from outside the perimeter.

Brenner's team would be supported by Rufus and ten more lion-shifters. As was the lion's way, they would go in armed to the teeth, and after initial contact, they would switch to were-mode and get down and dirty.

Grandma declined Griff's invitation to join them, as did Suki.

The Watcher's simply confirmed they would be observing.

Much to both Griff's and Max's chagrin, they were carried from the clan's property to the Quartet HQ, Brenner not trusting their innate human abilities to either keep up or remain undetected.

Brenner caried Griff, and Rufus did Max the dubious honor.

Then the shifters ensconced the two of them in a hastily erected hide some two hundred yards from the target, atop a small hill with a clear line of sight.

'Right,' said Brenner. 'Solomon, Michael and me will hit the North side. Rufus, you and yours hit the East. Griff and Max will start firing at any targets of opportunity while we advance. Questions?'

'Nah,' replied Rufus. 'Time to go fuck shit up.'

The two groups moved out, running at unbelievable speeds but making no sound at all.

Mere shadows in the night.

Chapter 54

Ivan Fedorov was not a racist. Simply put, he hated everyone. Even his fellow Russians. Especially his fellow Russians.

No, the reason he was arguing with Abeo Musa, the Nigerian leader of the African warrior team, was that Musa was obsessed with what he perceived as protocol.

Officers must be fed a higher class of food than the common soldiers. Enlisted men may not look an officer in the eye. Everyone who was not Abeo Musa himself, should behave with due deference and veneration when in his presence.

Fedorov had met men like this before. In fact, his own president was one. Men who considered themselves to be godlike. Beyond reproach.

But Fedorov also knew, these men were basically dickheads.

Just another reason to hate everyone.

'Listen, butt face,' snapped Fedorov. 'You will treat my men with respect. If you have a problem with any one of them, you will approach me first and I will deal with it. Understand?'

'Ha,' scoffed Musa. 'If you honestly think that for…'

The Nigerian paused, his eyes glazing over slightly as he tilted his head to one side.

As did Fedorov.

'Someone is coming,' they proclaimed in unison.

'We have a breach,' yelled Fedorov.

'To me, my warriors,' bellowed Musa.

All about the house men started running, some to the windows, others to prearranged vantage points. Yet more gathering around the leaders.

Specialist Zhao, the new Asian leader after Zobrondo had dispatched the previous one, ran up. 'I can feel two, maybe three separate groups,' he affirmed. 'But they feel odd. Not quite human.'

Before either of the other leaders could respond, the front windows of the house were rent asunder from a fusillade of automatic gunfire.

Some of the Quartet warriors returned fire.

Suddenly, an overwhelming amount of firepower crashed in from the East side of the building. Ten or more assault rifles and squad support weapons ripping thousands of rounds into the side of the building, smashing windows and tearing doors off their hinges.

'You and your men cover the front,' yelled Musa at Zhao. 'I will take the East, Ivan, you take the South.'

Fedorov nodded, all former arguments null and void as their professionalism overrode their personal feelings.

***

Zhao gathered his men and rushed to the front of the building. Using his enhanced sight, he scanned the surrounds and almost immediately spotted where the incoming fire was originating.

'Specialist Chen,' he called out. 'Eleven o-clock. Thirty-five degrees elevation. Looks like two or three shooters. Get six men to concentrate their fire there. I will attempt to flank their position with Wang and Li. Come on, you two, with me.'

Zhao and his team left the building via an exit on the West side, sprinting into the trees and then heading for Griff and Max's hide.

***

Musa and his men ran to the East of the building, keeping low as hundreds of steel jacketed rounds whipped and buzzed through the air. Whoever was firing at them obviously had no concerns about wasting ammo as they simply poured lead into the place.

Suddenly, the incoming stopped.

And the sound of automatic gunfire was replaced with something far worse.

Something primal.

Primitive and atavistic.

'What the hell is that?' yelled one of the men.

'I've heard that sound before,' answered Musa. 'In the Yankari Game Reserve back home. But that is impossible. It cannot be.'

'What?' asked one of the men.

'Lions.'

And out of the darkness they came, running impossibly fast. Each one standing seven feet plus. Canines like stilettos and claws like scythes.

'They are not lion,' whispered Musa, as his stomach cramped with superstitious terror. 'They are *Popobawa*. Lion-men.'

Musa managed to get off two shots before Rufus disemboweled him.

He had done better than the rest of his team.

***

Fedorov inched forward.

He couldn't see anything, but his every instinct was telling him to run. Or perhaps to just fall to the floor and grovel.

His fear was like a physical presence. Never before had he felt like this. Every breath an effort, sweat streamed down his face and his limbs felt weak. There was something out there, in the dark.

Something bad.

He turned to check on his men and saw they were in a worse state than him. Two of them were no longer even trying and had simply sat down.

Then he saw it.

The darkness exploded into light. A light so bright, and so frightening to his dark and evil soul that Fedorov instantly prostrated himself, gibbering in terror.

And from that light strode forth a being.

He was shrouded in Holy Fire. Silver wings graced his back, and in his right hand he carried a massive flaming broadsword.

On his right stood a creature straight out of the nightmares of our collective consciousness. Eight feet tall, four hundred pounds, eyes of burning gold. Teeth like bayonets and claws like daggers. Not man, but not a wolf.

And on his left, a man in black, red eyed, glistening canines, an expression of vague amusement on his pale face.

Then the wolfman stepped forward, grabbed Fedorov by the neck and yanked him to his feet.

And as those golden eyes bored into his very soul, Fedorov knew that he was staring into the Abyss.

Then the creature spoke, its voice mangled by its wolfish jaws. Not quite a growl, but still unlike any human speech.

It said one word, phrased as a question.

'Shadow?'

Fedorov whimpered.

'Shadow?' repeated the creature as he shook the Russian. 'Have you seen her?'

'No,' whispered Fedorov.

Brenner shook him one more time, but in the process, he inadvertently tore the Russian's head off.

'Fuck,' roared the wolfman as he strode over to the next combatant, picked him up and asked the same question.

Mere minutes later, there was no one left to ask.

***

Zhao and his men moved silently through the forest. Caution was more important than speed. He was determined to catch the enemy fireteam unaware.

Using hand signals only, he gestured for Wang and Li to flank wider, coming in from the opposite side to him. Pointing forward he urged them to move a little faster. He wanted them to hit first, then he would join. It would be a perfect pincer movement.

He could hear the gunfire continuing. The shooters were still ignorant of his approach.

Then Wang hit the tripwire.

Or perhaps it was Li.

Ultimately, it didn't really matter.

The two claymore mines detonated simultaneously.

One thousand four hundred steel balls traveling at over four thousand feet per second literally shredded the two Quartet warriors.

Before Zhao could react, his vision exploded and something struck the side of his head.

Rolling over, he looked up to see a middle-aged man in Vietnam era camouflage, holding an M16A1 assault rifle.

At first glance, the man had a kind face.

A favorite uncle, or maybe even a priest.

But if you looked closer you could see the thousand-yard-stare. The eyes of someone who has seen too much death, who has caused too much death.

The eyes of a killer.

Then the man spoke.

'Heard you coming from yesterday, dude,' he said. 'Man, I thought you were supposed to be good.'

Zhao said nothing, his dishonor at having been so helplessly outmaneuvered filled him with such shame he felt incapable of speech.

'Do you know where Shadow is?' the man with the kind face asked. 'Or anything about any women who has been taken prisoner by your organization, or any organization allied to yours.'

Griff's questioning was far more elucidating than Brenner's monosyllabic grunts.

But still, it reaped no reward.

'I am sorry,' replied Zhao. 'I do not understand.'

'Pity,' said the man.

Zhao never heard the shot that killed him.

Well, one never does.

Chapter 55

After Brenner's team had dispatched the entirety of the Quartet warriors and their servants, they had thoroughly searched the building for any information that might lead to Shadow.

But they found nothing.

'Dude,' said Griff as he sat down next to Brenner and handed him a lit cigarette. 'You okay?'

Brenner stared into the fire for a while before he answered.

'All this power,' he said. 'I mean, we went through fifty armed men and women, including thirty elite warriors with alleged supernatural abilities like they were a herd of turkeys. But can I find where Shadow is? No, not a hint. Don't even know if she's on the same planet. What's the point?'

'Hey, don't get down, we'll find her.'

'So everyone keeps saying,' sneered Brenner. 'We got angels, Watchers, Holy Knights, but not one of them can help find her. I call shenanigans. Someone must know where she is.'

'Someone does,' answered Griff. 'And when we find them, we'll find her. Hey, also, Shadow ain't no pushover. Odds are she'll break out on her own and find us.'

Brenner smiled. 'She just might,' he admitted.

'That's better,' said Griff.

'Hey, you two,' interjected Grandma. 'We got a problem.'

'Feel free to pile it on top of all the others,' said Brenner with a sigh. 'What's it now?'

'The Watchers have felt an incursion.'

'What's that?' asked Griff.

'A demon invasion, the likes of which they have not felt since pre-medieval times.'

'So, not good?' ventured Brenner.

Grandma shook her head. 'We're talking end of days shit here, big man,' she said.

'Wonder if any of them will know where Shadow is?' he mused.

'I'll give you one thing,' said Grandma in disbelief. 'You certainly have a one-track mind'

'Well, you know,' interjected Griff. 'Give the dog a bone and all that.'

'Not sure I get it,' frowned Grandma.

'Hey, is one of us meant to be a dog in this scenario?' growled Brenner.

The two Watchers walked over to join them. And for the first time ever, Brenner could see they were seriously concerned.

'Where is this invasion?' asked the big man.

'Detroit City,' answered mister Reeve.

'Size?'

'Hard to tell exactly, but from what we can feel, I would estimate the numbers to be in the high thousands. Mainly cacodemons, but also many demon lords. Perhaps even a couple of higher rank.'

'That's eight hours by car,' interjected Griff. 'Even if Suki manages to rustle up a helicopter or a jet, it's gonna be a few hours to get there.'

'We don't even have a few minutes,' stated mister Bolin.

'Well then we're screwed,' breathed Griff.

'No,' denied mister Reeve as he turned to Grandma. 'You can help us,' he said to her.

Grandma shook her head. 'It's too much. I don't have enough power.'

'We could help,' said mister Reeve.

'Really?' scoffed Grandma. 'Isn't that forbidden? The Watchers watch, they don't participate. Remember the Great Plan and all that shit.'

'It is a gray area,' said mister Bolin.

'No, it's not,' said Grandma.

'Let us say it is,' replied mister Bolin. 'For the sake of expediency.'

'What are you dudes talking about?' asked Griff.

'The Malak can open a portal; it is one of their specialties.'

'Yeah, for one or two beings. Not...' Grandma waved at the team and the clan members around her. 'Even with your help,' she added.

'Granted,' replied mister Bolin. 'But with our help you could take some. How many?'

'Wait,' interjected Griff. 'Is this going to cause you harm?' he asked Grandma. 'The way you dudes are talking I can tell this is some serious shit.'

Grandma shrugged. 'The process is not without danger.'

'Then I forbid it,' snapped Griff. 'No way. I couldn't take it if anything happened to you.'

Grandma leaned forward and stroked the old man's cheek.

'It is not up to you to allow or forbid an angel anything, human,' warned mister Reeve.

'Hey, Reeve,' said Grandma. 'Fuck you, if my man says I can't do it, then it's up to you to convince him otherwise. But you speak down to him again, you gonna need at least a gallon of that shine to stop yourself bleeding to death after I rip you a new asshole, understand?'

Mister Reeve frowned but did not argue back.

'Griff,' said mister Bolin. 'It is imperative that we go to Detroit. Thousands could perish if we do not stop the incursion. Hundreds of thousands even.'

'Don't care,' said Griff. 'Detroit's a shithole anyway. The Tigers can't hit a ball and the Lions haven't had a win since whenever.'

'So, half a million people must die because you do not favor their sports teams?' questioned mister Reeve angrily.

Grandma took Griff's hand. 'I have to try, you know that,' she informed him quietly.

Griff nodded. 'As long as I can come.'

'Of course,' agreed Grandma.

'How many can you handle?' asked mister Reeve.

Grandma thought for a while before she answered. 'Eight. At most.'

'Well, I'm in,' interjected Rufus. 'Any city that has a team called the Lions gets my vote.'

'They also have the Tigers,' added Suki.

'Fuck that,' scoffed Rufus. 'Tigers are fucking random.'

Brenner stood up. 'Griff, Solomon, Michael, Max, Rufus, the two misters, and me. Weapon up people, we leave ASAP.'

'And me?' asked Suki.

'Hey, I know you got skills,' answered Brenner. 'But they tend to lean more to the cerebral. Right now, we need dudes who are seriously good at fucking shit up.'

The big man could see Suki wanted to argue, but she was also reasonable enough to know he was right.

'Fine,' she conceded. 'I'll start organizing transport to get you out of there after you've finished fucking shit up.'

Solomon breathed an audible sigh of relief, happy that his partner was out of the danger zone.

Chapter 56

Zobrondo had been promoted by the council of infernals.

He was now a duke. And with the title he also gained his Name. With a capital N.

He was now officially known as Zobrondo the Soiled.

Asadak insisted it was cool.

Zobrondo wasn't so sure.

He would have preferred Mighty or even Cruel.

But you took what you got and you were eternally grateful.

Using his new rank, duke Zobrondo the Soiled had gathered together a corps of demon lords to assist him in his new attack.

The corps consisted of, Asadak, obviously, as he had been there from the start and, to be honest, which Zobrondo was not, it was initially his idea.

Plus, five others, Abdeel, Dagon, Ubel, Zagan and the female Usha.

Word on the street said there was a possibility the demon prince Nathotep, the stalker amongst the stars, might be joining them later. Zobrondo hoped the rumor was untrue, as quite frankly, he was shit scared of him.

All demon princes are assholes.

Psychotic, vicious assholes.

And prince Nathotep was widely regarded as the asshole in chief.

Between the corps of demon lords and himself, they had gathered up a herd of five thousand cacodemons as well a few hundred other minor demons including imps, incubi, succubae and asuras.

Zobrondo had set his incursion gateway to appear in the Vegan Foods Market. He figured it would be a great place to start possessing people, for no other reason than he couldn't stomach the whole meat-free idea.

After all, meat is meat and a demon must eat.

Preferably red, raw and bleeding.

On the other hand, duck is duck and a demon must ... eat poultry as well.

Whatever, he didn't like vegans.

Or vegetables.

The gateway crackled open and quickly expanded until it was wide enough to allow ten or fifteen cacodemons through at a time.

They flooded the area, cackling and screeching and ululating as they launched themselves at the milling throng of vegan victims, sucking their souls out and replacing them with the pure evil of the Lord of Lies.

Zobrondo and his fellow higher demons followed after a couple of hundred cacodemons had poured through, ensuring the way was both clear and safe.

The demon Duke saw the chaos around him and laughed long and loud.

Already, humans were attacking each other. Vegans tearing into one another's flesh with great glee and abandon. The irony of the whole spectacle adding vastly to Zobrondo's wicked pleasure.

He turned to his fellow demons, and was surprised to see, apart from Asadak, they were less amused and more nervous. In fact, their expressions were verging on panic.

'Hey,' he snapped. 'What's with the hang-dog looks. Does this not entertain?'

'It does,' admitted Usha. 'But, are you sure that the Watchers are no longer in the picture.'

'And Michael,' added Zagan as he gazed about in a fearful manner.

'And that fallen angel character, the Authority who is friends with the Malak,' interjected Dagon.

Zobrondo laughed scornfully. 'As Asadak and I have already assured you lightweights, we are sure the Watchers are no longer a problem. The veil is ours to cross with impunity. Michael? Fuck him. Brenner, that dog boy is a joke. And as for the Malak, since when did a lord cower from one of those?'

'Are you sure?' insisted Usha.

'Of course. Why do you keep asking?'

Usha pointed into the near distance. 'Because of that.'

Zobrondo turned to see a pillar of golden fire blaze skywards, and all about the sound of a heavenly choir filled the air.

And above it all, the roar of the Alpha of all alphas.

Brennerwolf.

'Oh, shit,' squealed Zobrondo. 'Shitty-shit-shit-fuckity-shit.'

Chapter 57

To avoid arriving amongst the general population, Grandma set her portal to open in the abandoned Packard factory on the east side of the city.

Almost four million square feet, at one stage employing over forty thousand workers, it is the largest abandoned factory in the world.

The portal crashed into existence. This was not Grandma's usual shimmering opening, capable of transporting one or perhaps two beings. This was a Watcher-enhanced monster, employing a raft of holy-power and transporting nine beings and their equipment over five hundred miles in the blink of an eye.

Golden fire blasted skywards to mark the portals opening, heavenly music echoed about the vast mausoleum of a factory, and every living plant within a hundred yards of the portal burst into flower.

The team did not need to step through the opening, they were simply there.

Michael gazed about and let out an exclamation of anguish. 'Woe and great sadness,' he cried. 'We are too late. The city has been totally destroyed. The apocalypse has begun.'

Griff shook his head and rolled his eyes. 'Man, you know, for an immortal holy-roller, you don't get out much. This is Detroit, dude, this is what it always looks like. Place is a shithole. Well, not completely,' he admitted. 'I mean, on the whole, the people are pretty cool, and they sure did improve music. Gotta love that Motown groove. And their Coney dogs are damned good. But apart from that, place is wall-to-wall Shits-ville.'

Mister Reeve pointed west. 'About two miles as the crow flies,' he said.

'What?' asked Brenner.

'The incursion. That is where they formed their doorway.'

'Well let's get on over there,' said Brenner. 'Come on,' he said to Griff. 'I'll carry you. Rufus can take Max.'

Griff shook his head. 'No. It's just too shameful, man. Being carried like a baby. Look, Max and I will hotwire a car as soon as we get out of this dead factory. We'll be a few minutes behind you at most.'

'Hey, Michael,' said Brenner.

'Yes.'

'What's the deadliest of the seven sins?'

'Pride.'

Brenner turned back to Griff. 'Hear that. Pride.'

'So?'

'So, you telling me you're too proud to be carried. Deadly sin, dude. You're screwing up our mission before we've even begun.'

'If it makes you feel any better,' interjected Michael. 'I shall carry you.'

Griff frowned. 'Now why should that make me feel better? Really, you know, sometimes you verge on being creepy. Damn it, fine. The big man can carry me.'

'Hey, Michael,' said Rufus. 'You mind carrying Max? I don't fucking like fucking carrying fucking people.'

Grandma chuckled. 'Rufus, after this is over, you and I are going to sit down and discuss adding a few more words to your vocabulary. You know, new verbs, some adjectives, maybe a couple of nouns.'

Rufus scowled. 'Yeah Grandma, whatever. Not actually sure what the fuck all those fucking things mean. Are we moving out or not?'

'We are,' affirmed Brenner. 'Michael, take Max. Griff, hop on my back, buddy.'

Griff pouted and did as he was told.

'Hey, Archangel,' said Solomon before they set off. 'I just want to make sure, is that aura of yours still going to protect me from the sun?'

Michael nodded. 'As long as you stay within a reasonable distance.'

'Clarify reasonable.'

'Fifty feet. At most. But if I were you, I would try to stay closer.'

'Bosom buddies,' quipped Solomon. 'Fine, let's go.'

Seconds later the team were heading towards the incursion point, moving at over forty miles an hour.

Three minutes later they stopped. Griff and Max were lowered to the ground and Griff immediately took out a pair of binoculars and scanned the surrounds.

'There,' he pointed. 'That's a children's hospital. Look, there's a whole crowd of what looks like zombies or some shit heading towards it.'

'Those aren't zombies,' said Grandma. 'They are the possessed.'

'Whatever they are,' said Griff. 'Some of them are eating other people, and in a few minutes they gonna be in the wards with all the little kiddies.'

'There's so many of them,' gasped Max. 'There must be thousands of the demons. And thousands of possessed. How can we possible stop this?'

'With difficulty,' said Brenner as he looked at the Watchers. 'Any advice.'

'You need to take out the demon lords. They control the cacodemons. You eliminate them, you destroy their minions.'

'Whatever we do,' interjected Griff. 'We better do it quick, because in a couple of minutes those zombie things are gonna be chowing down on children.'

'I shall stop them,' stated Michael, tearing his shirt off, spreading his wings and taking to the air, flaming sword held aloft.

'Well that means I'm also going,' added Solomon. 'Not that keen on suffering from terminal sunburn.'

He blurred into a run as he followed the Archangel.

'You two gonna help?' Brenner asked the Watchers.

'We shall watch.'

'Oh happy days,' scoffed the big man. 'Jubilation and euphoria.'

'We have already pushed the boundaries more than we should have,' interjected mister Bolin. 'And grade school level sarcasm will not change things.'

'I don't get it,' snapped Brenner. 'Just help. I know you got the power.'

'So do you,' said mister Reeve. 'And it is not for us to participate. That would be verging on meddling with free choice. It is your job to intercede. And when I say, your job, I mean that literally. You, Ded Brenner, are here for the sole purpose of fighting the good fight. And now you have a Malak, and an Archangel to help you.

'So quite bellyaching, count your blessings, and get out there and kick some demon ass.'

Griff chuckled. 'Consider yourself told off, dude.'

In the near distance next to the children's hospital, the team saw an explosion of golden light. This was followed immediately by a chorus of unearthly screams of agony.

'What is Michael doing?' asked Brenner.

'I would guess he is exterminating the afflicted and the cacodemons,' answered mister Reeve. 'Anything he thinks may harm the children.'

'So he's just killing the dudes who've been possessed?'

'Obviously,' answered mister Reeve.

'But they're human,' said Brenner.

'Not any more,' denied mister Reeve.

'They are innocent,' continued the big man. 'He is killing innocent people.'

'No, he is exterminating the infected. Sometimes hard choices must be made, Ded,' said mister Bolin.

'That's not fair,' said Brenner.

'I agree,' conceded mister Bolin. 'But unless you have a better way of doing things, that is all we have. And trust me, Michael is showing them a great mercy. Once they are possessed, their souls are imprisoned in their own personal hell.

'Pain, mental anguish, suffering beyond belief. Every foul deed they enact, every vicious murder, every obscene act, they feel it. They participate. Yet they can do nothing about it but rail hopelessly against the all-consuming torment their lives have become. Now go forth, Dark Angel,' continued mister Bolin. 'Exterminate the demon Lords, but be prepared to also release any poor possessed souls you come across. It is your destiny.'

'It's too much,' said Brenner.

'Yes,' agreed mister Reeve. 'Yet you still have to do it.'

Brenner took a deep breath, and then he nodded.

'Right,' he growled as he morphed into his wolfman mode. 'People, on me. Let's go take a look at this gateway and tear the living crap outa the bad guys.'

Chapter 58

'You promised,' whined Zagan. 'No Watchers, no Michael with his huge flaming sword. You gave us a guarantee.'

'Maybe it's not him,' ventured Zobrondo.

'You think?' scoffed Usha as she pointed at the being flying towards the children's hospital. 'No shirt, massive silver wings, six-foot-long flaming sword, looks like a combination of every male model who ever existed.'

There was an explosion of golden light as the archangel landed and began to smite all around him with great anger and furious vengeance.

'There seems to be someone else with him,' noted Asadak. 'A humanoid dressed in a black suit. Hellfire, whatever he is, he is fast.'

'At least the wolfman isn't here,' noted Zobrondo.

'Umm… my Duke,' interjected Dagon. 'We got incoming.'

Zobrondo looked up to see a group of people running towards them.

A wolfman, whom he assumed must be Brenner. A couple of humans, although they both gave off a weird vibe. Another human who seemed more animal than human. And the Malak.

'I vote we run away,' ventured Asadak. 'Our work here is done. Discretion being the better part of valor and all that crap.'

'Yep, he who fights and runs away, lives to fight another day,' added Zagan.

'Rather a live coward than a dead hero,' quipped Usha.

'Steady on,' reacted Asadak. 'It's not cowardly, it's a strategic withdrawal.'

'Yeah,' interjected Zobrondo. 'Tactics. We are definitely not just running away.'

'Consolidating,' suggested Ubel.

'Whatever we want to call it,' snapped Asadak. 'Can we all just get outa here?'

'Me first,' shouted Zobrondo as he sprinted for the open gateway.

But before he could get there, a sound akin to the smashing of a million glass window panes, followed by a crack of rolling thunder rent the air. A series of explosions followed.

And the gateway came crashing down, disappearing in a swirling cyclone of light and dark.

'Oh, shit,' squealed Zobrondo for the second time. 'Shitty-shit-shit-fuckity-shit.'

***

'There,' yelled Grandma as they neared the gateway. 'Those ugly SOB's standing by the RV. Demon lords. Those are the ones controlling the cacodemons. We kill them, we can stop this.'

'Shit,' cussed Griff. 'Looks like they're trying to make a break.'

Grandma pointed her staff at the gateway, concentrated, and fired a pulse of energy.

An actinic bolt of light struck the gateway with a sound like a giant gong, reverberating the buildings, shaking the ground and substantially reducing the size of the portal.

'Griff,' shouted Brenner. 'Chuck me a couple of grenades.'

Griff complied, pulling the pins and tossing the live grenades to Brenner who caught them and launched them over four hundred yards with unerring accuracy. They exploded against the gateway, further reducing its size.

'Max,' continued Brenner. 'More.'

The Knight obeyed, chucking another brace of M67's over. These followed the last pair.

Then Grandma hit the gateway again, and with a sound like a mountain of smashing crystal, it disintegrated into a swirling mess of black dust and motes of light.

'Now let's ice these uglies,' yelled Griff.

'Careful,' warned Grandma. 'They may be cowardly, but when cornered they can be vicious as all hell. Do not underestimate them. They are near the pinnacle of demonic power. Particularly that one,' she pointed at Zobrondo. 'If I am not mistaken, he appears to be a Duke, and I am afraid I have little power left after transporting us here and then helping to take down that gateway.'

'No worries, Grandma,' growled Brennerwolf. 'He's mine. The rest of you, take out the others.'

And like an inferno of holy fire, the team fell upon them.

Chapter 59

Solomon had been alive for a very long time. He had fought in over seven known major wars, and many undercover ones. The type that never made the newspapers.

He had seen death in all of its guises, and he had killed more human beings than anyone should.

He had fought titans, hybrid monsters, special forces agents and more.

But, apart from Brenner in his Dark Angel mode, he had never come across a force as destructive, and as terrifyingly cataclysmic as Michael in full force.

His flaming sword moved so fast as to appear as a solid sphere of fire. And when he swung, it's length extended to over a hundred feet, destroying all in its path.

Hundreds of possessed fell before his mighty blade as it burned them in twain.

When the holy fire struck one of the cacodemons, it caused them great and obvious pain, sending them into screeching paroxysms of fear and rage.

But it did not kill them. The only way to dispatch their evil was to exterminate the humans that had been possessed by them.

Wholesale murder of the innocent.

Solomon joined in, blurring from possessed to possessed. Using his supernatural strength to rip their heads from their bodies as he attempted to put them out of their misery as quickly and humanely as possible. Even though it sickened him.

He glanced across at the Archangel and was shocked to see him laughing almost hysterically as he killed again, and again, and again.

But as Solomon drew closer to him, he could plainly see that Michael was not laughing.

In fact, he was weeping.

Unconsolably.

Every cut he made; every life he took brought fresh tears to his eyes.

Solomon could hear him mumbling under his lamentations.

'And lo, shall I defend you in battle. I shall be your protection against the wickedness and snares of the devil. By the power of God, I shall cast into hell Satan and all the evil spirits who prowl about the world seeking the ruin of souls. God forgive me for what I do, in his name.'

To see such dedication, such selflessness and such belief, humbled Solomon.

And he turned back to his awful task with renewed vigor.

Chapter 60

'Max, with me,' shouted Griff. 'Rufus, flank left. Grandma, stay back for now. Ded, go fuck shit up.'

Brennerwolf howled his anger as he made a beeline for the largest demon, the one Grandma had singled out as a possible Duke of hell.

The other five demons split into two groups, snarling and spitting as they readied themselves for an attack.

Griff and Max had forgone their usual choice of weapon, *id est*, an assault rifle and a SAW, for a brace of AA-12 automatic 12-gauge shotguns, with 32-round magazines.

The package was a little bulky, but the massive rate of fire and the fact they each carried another couple of drum magazines made up for the bulk.

Rufus carried an M16A1 assault rifle in his left hand and an M32 semi-auto grenade launcher in his right. His shifter enhanced strength made it possible to be able to wield both weapons at the same time. As was his clan's habit, he tended to use his weapons first, and then drop them when he got up close and personal. Changing into his hybrid mountain lion mode in order to rend and tear.

Max and Griff opened fire first, both shotguns on full auto, spewing out a combined total of ten rounds of double-aught a second. The ordnance rocked the one group of two demons back on their heels. Surprisingly, the rounds did not do as much damage as Griff was hoping.

Rufus joined in next, targeting the trio of demons on the left. His combination of 5.56 millimeter high-velocity rounds plus the 40-millimeter grenades did a little more damage than the shotguns. The slugs penetrating deeper, and the grenades actually throwing the three demons back a few steps.

Brennerwolf and Zobrondo smashed into each other like a pair of runaway trains. The earth shook and a shockwave punched out from the point of contact. Both were traveling so fast the sound of their collision was like an explosion.

Zobrondo was huge, and toughened by the fires of hell and the evil powers of his master.

But Brennerwolf was … well, Brenner.

And whereas Zobrondo was built for evil and malevolence and general acts of nastiness, Brenner's sole purpose was to fight.

To be honest, Zobrondo was surprisingly resilient. His hide was almost impervious to Brennerwolf's claws, and his rate of self-healing was off the charts. As fast as Brenner broke things, Zobrondo healed them.

Limbs, ruptured eyeballs, torn off ears.

And in return, the demon's talons were enhanced with hell-fire, and his bite was at least a thousand times more toxic than a rattlesnake.

Rufus concentrated his fire on the middle demon, hitting him with all six M40 grenades and most of the thirty rounds of FMJ from the M16.

He didn't know, but he had directed his fire at one of the demon lords formerly known as, Ubel.

Now, he would be more appropriately referred to as, dead.

Due to Rufus's shifter enhanced strength and natural weapons skills, almost every round, including the grenades, had impacted Ubel's cranium.

And as such, it pretty much no longer existed.

'Idiot,' screeched the female, Usha, a sneer of scorn twisting her demonic appearance as she contemplated Rufus. 'Now you're out of ammunition. Prepare to die.'

'Fuck you,' cussed Rufus. 'Anyway, I'm fucking bored of guns, it's time to get jiggy with you fuckers.'

And he exploded into his hybrid mountain lion form. Four hundred pounds of snarling, razor clawed pissed. Without any further preamble, he attacked. A roaring, spitting ball of absolute fury.

Griff and Max were fighting on the back foot, covering each other as they walked slowly backwards, tagging the pair of demons again and again.

'Reloading,' yelled Griff.

'Firing,' stated Max as he put short burst of double-aught into the advancing pair of demons.

'Grenade,' interjected Griff as he tossed an M62 frag at the demons.

'Reloading,' shouted Max.

'Firing,' affirmed Griff.

The contest wasn't exactly a stalemate, initially the demons were most definitely getting the worst of the altercation, as round after round of 12 gauge slammed into them, enhanced with the odd fragmentation grenade.

The sheer weight of firepower was not only beginning to overtake their capacity to self-heal, it was also preventing them from closing with their enemy. And unless they were able to get up close, they had little chance of doing any harm.

'Where is Shadow?' growled Brenner as he launched another punch at Zobrondo, clubbing him in the chest with enough power to destroy a Mack truck.

The demon duke took a step back, the sound of his ribs breaking audible even above the ordnance Griff and Max were unloading close by.

'Ah yes, the mother of the Messenger,' said Zobrondo.

'Where?' roared Brenner as he stepped forward, blocking a kick from the demon and counter attacking with a slashing left jab that punctured the evil creature's eyeball with a sickening pop.

Zobrondo screamed in pain, staggering backwards to escape Brenner's implacable advance. 'I do not know,' he yelled. 'I am but a Duke. Only a Prince of the realm would be privy to such information.'

'Liar,' thundered Brenner as he struck again, smashing the bones in Zobrondo's face to pulp.

'Merk har groodle,' garbled Zobrondo, unable to form words due to the fact his jaw was now more bone chips than actual jawbone. Also, the complete lack of teeth didn't help.

'Hey, Ded,' yelled Griff. 'We're taking strain here. These douche canoes are tougher than a pair of Texan grannies. Gonna need some help ASAP. Even Rufus is struggling.'

'Busy,' snapped Brenner as he grabbed Zobrondo and proceeded to rip one of his wings off. 'Talk to me,' he bellowed.

Zobrondo squealed in terrified pain. 'I don't know,' he shrieked.

Brenner shook the demon back and forth in an effort to dislodge some information from him. Anything at all.

But in his anger, he didn't notice the demon duke slide a jagged, black, poison coated blade from a scabbard on his hip.

With a grunt of effort, Zobrondo struck hard, punching the wicked, vicious looking blade deep into Brenner's gut.

The pain imparted by the dark-blade was beyond imagining as it released a bolt of evil energy into Brenner's torso, burning and tearing his organs apart as it did so.

Zobrondo withdrew the blade and struck again.

But this time, Brenner caught the demon's wrist, twisting and snapping his arm. The dagger dropped to the floor and Brenner stepped back, clutching his wound, breathing heavily, struggling to stay on his feet.

'Dude,' yelled Griff. 'We're in the shit here. You gonna have to hulk out man. Let's see the wings. The attitude. Come on.'

'Doesn't work like that,' gasped Brenner. 'If it did, I'd already be doing it.'

Rufus staggered back from his two remaining opponents, he was severely wounded, but on the whole, he was probably winning. Both the demon lords facing him were on their last legs.

But to be fair, so was Rufus.

'I fucking hate demons,' he grunted. 'Ugly fucking, smelly, useless pieces of crap.'

Meanwhile, Zobrondo used Brenner's temporary setback to turn and run, looking for some place to recover from his horrific wounds.

But Brennerwolf was having none of that. Roaring out his anger and pushing through the pain, he pursued the demon duke, tackling him like a Dallas Cowboy lineman. The two of them went down in a tangle of limbs and wings and claws and teeth, snapping and growling and tearing at each other.

Max emptied his last magazine of double-aught, dropped his shotgun and drew his 45.

'I'm all out,' he shouted as he double tapped the closest demon while walking backwards in an attempt to stay away from its teeth and talons.

Rufus went down as his remaining two demon lords managed to heal up enough to put in a concerted attack. The three of them rolled around on the floor, beating on each other like contestants in a pro-wrestling death match.

Max threw his empty 45 at one of the demons and took out his KA-BAR combat knife, ready to fight to the last.

Griff ran out of ammo at the same time.

Grandma stepped forward, her staff held high, but Griff could see she was still exhausted from her previous efforts, and he knew she would be lucky to generate enough power for a single bolt of light. Not enough to do more than piss the demons off.

They had all fought well, but as Grandma had warned them, demon lords were not to be taken lightly. They were big, they were bad and they were gifted with extra power by Beelzebub himself.

But as the two demons lunged forward, Brenner stepped in front of them, clubbing both to the floor with a left and a right.

'Nick of time, buddy,' quipped Griff as he turned to see if there was any possible help he might give Rufus, but there was no need. In a blinding flash of golden light, Michael appeared, flaming sword in hand.

Microseconds behind him, Solomon arrived.

And then the fat lady must have sung – because it was all over.

The already badly wounded demons were no match for the fresh Archangel and the man in black who literarily tore them apart.

Brenner rushed over to Zobrondo who was still clinging precariously to life and asked him one last time about Shadow.

The demon duke smiled; the smashed stumps of his teeth covered in blood.

'Fuck you,' he gasped. 'And the horse you rode in on,'

Brenner snapped his neck.

And all around them, the remaining possessed fell to the ground. Some, lifeless, others twitching and fitting as their mortal minds attempted to recover from the hellish nightmare they had just endured.

Some would survive.

Many wouldn't.

Still more would finish the remainder of their lives as little more than burned out husks. Trapped inside an endless darkness.

But the incursion was over.

And who knows, perhaps Detroit would now actually be able to follow their motto?

Speramus meliora; resurget cineribus.

'We hope for better things; it shall arise from the ashes.'

Perhaps.

But most likely not.

'Brenner,' yelled Grandma.

'What?'

'I can feel her,' answered Grandma. 'Shadow. She's free.'

Chapter 61

The thunder rolled, and the lightning struck.

And the lion was set free, rising from the depths of her unconscious mind. Ready to fight. Ready to run.

Ready to deal some damage.

Shadow roared her anger as she smashed her demon guard into the bars, using her claws to sever his head from his shoulders.

Taking the keys from his belt, she opened the gate and prowled down the dark stone corridor. Smoky torches guttered in rusted metal sconces, and the stink of brimstone and rotting flesh filled the air.

The corridor split and she was faced with a choice. Remembering something she had once heard about mazes, Shadow decided to keep going right. After a few steps she hesitated, was it left? Right?

'Crap,' she mumbled to herself. 'Doesn't matter, just keep moving.'

After a few yards she ran straight into another demon. Grabbing him by the throat, and driving her claws into his neck she growled. 'Where is the exit?'

The demon struggled for a few seconds, then realized it was totally outmatched, so it pointed. 'There,' it croaked. 'Take the first left. Second right, keep going. You can't miss it.'

Shadow frowned. She didn't believe the demon, but sometimes even a bad plan is better than no plan at all.

'Are you going to kill me?' asked the hell spawn.

Shadow nodded.

'Ah, shit.'

Shadow slashed her claws sideways, slicing through the creature's jugular. Then she dropped it, letting it bleed out as she continued on her way.

Surprisingly, the demon had told her the truth, and mere minutes later she was standing outside, on a snow-covered mountaintop, the wan sun trickling through the pine trees and dappling the snow with lacy patterns of light and shade.

Shadow took a deep breath. The first proper fresh air she had taken in for a while.

Then she smiled.

'How very clever of you.'

Shadow spun around to see a demon.

But this wasn't like any hell spawn she had laid eyes on before. It was obvious this was no normal demon.

He stood over ten feet tall. His skin a deep burgundy, shot through with flashes of bright red, like veins of lava in volcanic rock.

On his head a set of massive horns curled on either side, meeting his ears. Shadow could see they were razor sharp.

His eyes glowed with red fire, and his muscles stood out like he was cast from molten steel.

And his voice was like none she had heard before. A stunning basso profundo. Barry White on his best day. But with it came an exquisite sense of beauty, of yearning. A need to bathe in its magnificence.

It took all of Shadow's phenomenal mental strength to resist the siren call of the demon's voice.

'And you were so close,' it continued. 'I mean, of course I could have stopped you earlier. But to do so now, when you truly thought you had escaped, well, that is all the more delicious.'

Shadow tensed up, readying herself for battle.

The demon laughed. The sound a genuinely heart-warming sound. The chuckle of a favorite uncle at Christmas. A parent's loving laughter, a lover's smiling embrace.

Because true evil is not ugly. It is beautiful. It is seductive. It is powerful.

The serpent's skin patterned in jeweled colors. The ethereal construct of a Black Widows web. The petals of a poisonous orchid.

'Do not be stupid, child,' said the demon. 'Do you have any idea who I am?'

'Don't care,' snapped Shadow. 'You want to kill my child, and I will not allow that. So whoever you are, come and get some, you son of a bitch.'

Again, the demon chuckled. 'I am prince Nathotep,' he said. 'I sit at the right hand of the Father of Darkness. You have as much chance of besting me as a gnat has of crushing an elephant. Do yourself and your unborn child a favor, turn around and go back to your cell. Now.'

'Fuck you,' cussed Shadow. 'I'd rather die. So, as I already said, come and get some, asswipe.'

Chapter 62

The portal tore open a doorway, punching through dimensions in time and space in order to transport Brenner to his destination.

Grandma had barely enough power to open the doorway, so once again the Watchers had helped. But even their prodigious powers were running low. As a result, Brenner came alone.

But that was fine with him.

He had come to get Shadow, and woe betide any SOB who tried to stop him.

As he stepped through the opening, he staggered slightly, the wound from the hell-cursed dagger still effecting his system. The combination of the poisons and the dark curses proving difficult to heal.

He was weakened. But he was pissed.

It took the big man all of two seconds to get his bearing, and then he saw her.

In her hybrid lion mode. Standing proud, claws extended and teeth bared.

Opposite her, a massive demon.

Brenner frowned as the demon's obvious power washed over him. This was no common and garden variety demon. This asswipe was seriously bad news.

Shadow turned to look at him, and the expression of love and relief and absolute trust made his heart swell.

'You took your time,' she growled with a grin.

'Sorry,' apologized Brenner. 'Traffic was a bitch.'

'Marvelous,' crowed prince Nathotep. 'Sometimes I can't believe my luck. The infamous Ded Brenner. Fallen angel attempting to claw his way out of the Darkness. I must admit, you are not nearly as impressive as I expected you to be.'

'Who's this douche bag?' Brenner asked Shadow.

'Just some demon with delusions of grandeur,' answered Shadow. 'Do me a favor, lover, and rip his head off so we can go home.'

'Sure thing,' acknowledged Brenner.

Without any warning at all, the big man attacked, blurring across the intervening space and slamming into the demon prince like a runaway train.

Snow shivered from the surrounding trees, and the earth shook as the two titans collided in an explosion of sound and fury.

But to Brenner's surprise and dismay, Nathotep didn't budge. It was like running into a granite cliff face.

'Pathetic,' sniffed Nathotep. 'After all the stories I was hoping for a Superman, instead I got Pinocchio.' He stepped forward and struck Brennerwolf in the chest.

The blow sounded like an axe striking a giant Redwood. The sheer force of it drove Brenner back at least ten feet.

The big man counterattacked, but the prince of hell slipped his twin punches, lashing out with his foot in return and sweeping Brenner to the ground.

Brenner immediately sprung back to his feet and attacked again, a whirlwind of punches and bites. A few hits got through but they hardly seemed to phase the huge demon who retaliated by delivering a stunning back roundhouse kick to the wolfman's neck.

Brenner staggered sideways as a jagged pain ripped through his body, the vertebrae in his neck barely standing up to the massive strike.

Shadow threw caution to the wind when she saw the love of her life taking such punishment. She jumped on Nathotep's back, clawing at his eyes and biting the back of his head.

But with almost contemptuous ease, the demon prince grabbed her and threw her into a pine tree, shattering her ribs and breaking her back.

'No,' roared Brenner as he ran towards her.

But before he could reach her, Nathotep was on top of him, hammering at him with savage, controlled blows that crushed flesh and broke bones.

'Time to die, little doggy,' proclaimed Nathotep as he extended his talon and readied himself to remove Brenner's head.

'In your dreams, hellboy,' grunted Brenner.

The air shimmered as a wave of unearthly power burst forth from the big man.

A deep bass note rocked the land, trees exploded as their sap boiled, rocks shattered, filling the air with deadly shards of shrapnel, and the snow around them began to steam, creating a thick fog that settled over the entire area.

And from out of the fog came the fallen angel.

Brenner.

Wolf.

Angel.

Vengeance.

Twenty feet tall, with wings that spanned over sixty feet.

And lo, the firmament above rang with the sound of rejoicing.

At the same time, it was filled with the sound of terror. The gibbering and mewling of the unrighteous.

For the angel of darkness had risen from the abyss to claim what was rightfully his.

To seek redemption.

To recover hope.

To reap the whirlwind.

There was no anger. No outrage. There was simply judgement.

And the instrument of that judgement was Brenner.

Thus did the dark angel lean down and grasp the demon prince, picking him up and studying him.

Nathotep struggled frantically, but it was to no avail. Because he had been weighed, he had been measured, and he had been found wanting.

With a mere shrug of his shoulders and a tensing of his forearms, the dark angel reduced the demon to little more than a handful of crushed and broken flesh.

Dropping the remains to the ground, the angel stepped upon it, grinding it into the earth until there was naught left but a stain.

A mere blemish on the pristine snow.

'Brenner.'

The angel of the abyss did turn and inspect the tiny human that had dared approach it.

'It's over,' said the mortal. 'Come back to me.'

Shadow held her hand out.

Suns rose and set. Some went supernova, some merely guttered to blackness. Galaxies expanded, and ages passed in an instant. Worlds died and were reformed and time stopped, and began again.

All in the blink of an eye.

'Shadow?'

'Yes.'

And Brenner was back.

Chapter 63

'So, the Great Plan,' said Brenner. 'What exactly does it involve? Also, if I'm an integral part of it, shouldn't I have been consulted? Or at very least been told about it.'

Michael frowned. 'Firstly, no one knows exactly what the Great Plan entails,' he answered. 'All we can be sure about, is that it is ineffable. Should you have been consulted? No. Why weren't you told about it? Well, you were, when you needed to know.'

'What happened to free choice?' argued Brenner.

'I don't understand,' admitted Michael.

'If I didn't know about being part of the plan, how could I choose whether or not I wanted to be part of it?'

'Are you saying that your choices would be different?' interjected mister Reeve. 'You would have chosen not to defend the weak, to help the righteous, to do good?'

'Obviously not,' answered Brenner.

'Well then quit bellyaching,' said mister Reeve. 'You done good. All's well that ends well, and other such meaningless platitudes.'

'And my daughter?' asked Shadow. 'How does she fit into this Great Plan?'

'She is destined to be the Messenger,' said Grandma.

Shadow shrugged. 'Yeah, the demons kept saying that. Not sure what it means.'

'Firstly,' said Grandma. 'You need to know that the word Angel derives from the Greek *Angelos*, a translation of the Hebrew word, Messenger.'

'My daughter is an Angel,' gasped Shadow.

Griff chuckled. 'Don't know why you're so surprised, after all, Ded is an Authority. Kinda makes you wonder how low they set the bar on these things.'

Grandma laughed. 'The key word in all of this is, ineffable. Which is just another way, sweetheart, of saying, maybe. Or who knows. But what we do know is, if she does grow up to be the Messenger, she will achieve great power. She shall become enlightened, part of the very fabric of all that is, that has been and what shall come.

'In ages past, the Messenger was oft referred to as, the Peace Bringer. She will see all, help the world to communicate, tear down the barriers. Or not, we shall have to wait and see.'

Grandma patted Shadow on the shoulder. 'Whatever is going to happen, rest assured, your child will be strong, healthy, well loved and well protected. And that is enough.'

'And me?' asked Brenner. 'What do I do now?'

'What do you want to do?' asked mister Bolin.

Brenner shrugged. 'Nothing really. Rest. Smoke. Have breakfast. Not fight demons. Protect my family. Live.'

The Watchers stood up together.

'Then do that,' said mister Bolin with a smile. 'After all, you deserve a break. Go home to Backlash. Be the sheriff. Or don't. Your life is yours to live.'

'And thank you,' added mister Reeve. 'For all you have done.'

'What about money?' interjected Griff. 'You say do whatever you want, but how can he? He's gotta work for a living.'

Mister Reeve raised an eyebrow. 'If he needs money, he need only ask the Malak.'

Griff turned to Grandma. 'Really? You said you got money before, but exactly how much are we talking?'

Grandma laughed. 'Enough,' she said. 'Actually, more than enough. Put it this way, the Messenger won't have to worry about starting a college fund. Or buying a house. Or a bunch of houses. Or her own country.'

'If you so rich, then how come we live in a two-bedroom log cabin in the forest in the middle of nowhere?'

'Where would you like to live?' asked Grandma.

Griff scowled. 'That's not the point,' he said.

'What is the point, then?' asked Grandma.

Griff chuckled. 'Nothing. No point. Sorry.'

'Hey, Suki,' said Brenner. 'Is it possible to organize us some transport? I wanna go home.'

Suki nodded. 'Sure thing, big man.' She turned to Max. 'And you, what's you plan of action?'

Max shrugged. 'To be perfectly honest, I didn't expect to be alive at the end. Papa even gave me the last rites. I'm at a bit of a loose end.'

'Hang around with us for a while,' said Suki. 'Take a break. Think. Whatever you need, just ask.'

Max nodded his thanks.

Shadow walked over to Brenner and put her arms around him.

He smiled down at her.

And everything was good again.

Epilogue

The head of the African cabal of the Quartet swore softly and stabbed at his keyboard again.

After the debacle of the last meeting, where the Asian leader had insisted they used magical communications as opposed to Zoom, a vote had been taken. And the general consensus was, magic sucks.

So, they had voted to resort to the Zoom model of meeting once more.

But for some reason, he was unable to raise anyone at the scheduled time.

'Hello,' he yelled ineffectually at his microphone. 'Where the hell are you imbeciles? Anyone? We had a meeting arranged.'

'He's not the sharpest tool in the box,' said mister Reeve.

'Most definitely not,' agreed mister Bolin as he poured himself a shot of shine.

The African leader spun around. 'What the…? Who the hell are you two? And how did you get into this room? And where did that table come from? I never had a table in here before. This is impossible.'

'No,' disagreed mister Reeve. 'Impossible would denote the said happening was not able to occur. And as it patently has, I would offer to you that you are misusing the word. Perhaps you meant, unlikely.'

The leader pulled a pistol from the drawer in his desk. 'Oh yes, very clever,' he yelled. 'Let's see how clever you are when I shoot you in the face. Now, I ask again, who the fuck are you?'

'No need for the gun,' said mister Bolin. 'All you need do is ask.'

'I just did.'

True,' admitted mister Reeve. 'Well, in that case, we are the Watchers.'

The leader staggered backwards and fell into his chair. 'Impossible,' he gasped.

'There he goes again with that word,' noted mister Reeve. 'The fellow has no real grasp of the English language.'

'And after we just explained it to him,' added mister Bolin with a frown.

The leader raised his pistol again and pointed it with a shaking hand. 'I know the rules,' he said. 'You can't do anything to me. It's all part of the Great Plan. You Watch, nothing more, nothing less.'

Mister Reeve poured himself another shot of shine and tossed it back. 'You are correct,' he acknowledged.

'However,' interjected mister Bolin. 'We have decided, just this one time, to extend our remit.'

The implication of the sentence mister Bolin had just uttered slowly dawned on the leader.

'That's not allowed,' said the leader.

'True,' admitted mister Reeve. 'It is unusual. But not entirely unheard of. In fact, I might even say that we have set some sort of a trend very recently.'

'The rest of the Quartet members,' said the leader. 'I can't contact them because they are all dead. You killed them.'

Mister Reeve gave the man a slow clap. 'Exactly,' he affirmed. 'Well done.' He turned to mister Bolin. 'And you said he wasn't that bright.'

'Actually, I think that was you,' contradicted mister Bolin.

Mister Reeve nodded. 'You may be correct.'

The leader squeezed the trigger of his semi-automatic, cranking out seven rounds.

They had no effect on either of the Watchers. In fact, the slugs simply dropped to the floor as soon as the exited the barrel.

'Now that wasn't very nice,' noted mister Reeve.

'I concur,' agreed mister Bolin.

'What now?' whispered the leader.

'Now?' said mister Reeve. 'Now, you die.'

And the last of the Quartet members slumped to the floor as his head exploded with a dull thump.

'And that,' said mister Reeve. 'I believe, is that.'

****

Hi guys – thanks for reading and sticking with Brenner for so long.

Is this the end? Well, I wouldn't say that. After all, the Messenger promises to have a story of her own.

But for now – I'm onto The Forever Man.

Then a new series – The Hammer of the Gods.

And finally …

If you want to sign up for my newsletter and get a FREE Novella – just hit the link below. Join the tribe and have great fun with giveaways, free short stories, audio books and loads of news…

https://BookHip.com/QSLPAHD

Thanks again for all.

Your friend in words

Craig

PS If you want to give me a shout to discuss anything, please feel free to email me at…
craig@craigzerf.com

I'll get straight back to you.

 If you want to sign up for my newsletter and get a FREE Novella – just hit the link below. Join the tribe and have great fun with giveaways, free short stories, audio books and loads of news…

https://BookHip.com/QSLPAHD